RED RUNES OF CHINA

H . BEDFORD-JONES

RED RUNES OF CHINA

H. BEDFORD-JONES

ALTUS PRESS • 2016

© 2016 Altus Press • First Edition—2016

EDITED AND DESIGNED BY
Matthew Moring

PUBLISHING HISTORY
"Red Runes of China" originally appeared in the April 10–June 25, 1924 issues of *Short Stories* magazine (Vol. 107, Nos. 1–6).

THANKS TO
Rebecca Burns, Richard Hall, Everard P. Digges LaTouche, Gerd Pircher and Chris Slembarski

TABLE OF CONTENTS

I

THE CHOW CHARACTER

*The Runes Told of Mystery, of Danger Lurking
in Odd Corners, of the Craft of the Orient Put
to Evil Purposes in the Far West, and Started
Young Dick Clews on a Great Adventure*

T HAT CRYPTIC clue in the Vanderhoof diamond case was interwoven with logic and sheer chance. It was natural that I should go home to Friedman with it, yet it was by purest luck that we were not involved in the publicity. It so happened that in all the teeming life of San Francisco, Lew Friedman did not have a friend outside myself, nor I one except for him. His very existence was unknown, and for this highly important fact there was a reason.

Three weeks before the Vanderhoof affair, I had met Lew again after losing sight of him for three years and more. I was trying to hold down a newspaper job in this city where I was absolutely unknown; and I wanted to stay unknown. I did not care to advertise that Dick Clews, former star athlete, soldier of fortune, and officer in the Chinese army, was down and out. One afternoon I was running down a story in Millard Street, one of those short, rear hillside streets of San Francisco, when I was astounded to hear my name called in a woman's clear and penetrating voice.

"Captain Clews! Captain Clews! Please step here a moment!"

Dumbfounded, I turned to see a trained nurse standing on the veranda of a house across the street and beckoning.

When I crossed over, she addressed me smilingly. "Mr. Friedman asked me to call you over—he saw you from the window."

"Friedman—Lew Friedman?" I answered, and went up the steps two at a time.

We had been good friends in Tientsin. Lew Friedman had done me many a good turn when I was a griffin, as a tenderfoot is termed in China, for in those days he was an adviser to the government, a former college professor, who knew everything in and about China.

The nurse ushered me into a silent house, and then into a large, sunny room overlooking the street. The room was filled with books, but my eyes were all for the man in the wheelchair by the window. Lew Friedman was a pitiful shadow of his old self, a wreck of a man; though he was not yet sixty, his power-ful, leonine head was crowned by snowy hair. Yet the great blue eyes were vigorous, clear, luminous as ever.

"Dick!" He reached out a hand to me. "Could hardly believe my eyes when I saw you climbing the hill! Looking for me?"

"Hadn't a notion you were here," I said. "What's the trouble? Sick?"

A smile came to his lips—a brave one.

"Had my spine injured two years ago, been here ever since," he said, leaning back on his pillows. "All alone except for two nurses and a cook. Sit down, sit down! What army are you serving in now?"

"I'm reporting for the *Star*, temporarily. Lord, but I'm glad to see you! Not like this, though. Two years, eh? You don't mean that it's permanent?"

"Permanent, and I'm lucky to be alive. I'm able to sit up a few hours each day and work at Chinese translation—you needn't look so shocked, either. I've lived my life, Dick, and I'm not whining. So chuck it. Tell me all about yourself. Married?"

"No chance," I returned, and settled down to talk. It was hard to realize that this man was a cripple; in the old days he was as good as the best of us, either with brains or brawn, and better than most with brains. Still, here was he and here was I, and we had a great gam until the nurse turned me out.

Both of us were lonely men, liking one another rarely; so in the course of a fortnight I moved into an upper room of Friedman's house, and our old friendship had a chance to reach intimacy once more, which it speedily did. So that was the status of affairs when the Vanderhoof story broke and changed the whole course of my life.

II

THE VANDERHOOF affair was a police case, which was why it fell to me; one of the dicks who was an ex-marine, tipped me off, and I went out with the brace of them. There was at first sight nothing markedly sensational about the case. Vanderhoof's apartment was near the cable car barns in California Street.

He was a plump, straightforward little Hollander, a broker in diamonds, and told a straight story. He and his wife lived alone. He came home to lunch, bringing some stones which he was to take to a prospective customer at two that afternoon. During luncheon, two men came to the door, asked for him, and calmly held him up. They tied him and his wife in two chairs, took his stones, and decamped. The loot was valued at $10,000.

I kept quiet, while the detectives got busy. Description? Both holdup men were well dressed, fairly young, dark of complexion, without distinguishing features. Fingerprints? They wore rubber gloves, which did not interfere with handling a pistol. Nothing but the stones was taken; they knew exactly what they wanted, took it, and vanished.

"Inside job, either from your end or the other," commented one dick. "Got any clerks?"

Vanderhoof had one confidential assistant in his Grant Street office; could not say whether the man was aware of the stones taken home, but trusted the clerk implicitly. What about the other end, then? Who was the customer?

"Harvey Blake," said Vanderhoof, and the dicks looked at each other blankly.

It was a well known name. Harvey Blake was a millionaire of expensive habits but excellent reputation, and could be at once discounted. As a matter of form, one of the dicks went off to interview him, the other stayed to look around the place, and so did I. There was not a single clue, except the cord used to tie up Vanderhoof and his wife. It was fine, strong, thin cord, half silk, and appeared to be Chinese.

I was at the doorway, hat in hand, when I glanced back and saw a scrap of paper at the dining-room entrance. With all a cub reporter's eagerness, I went back and picked it up; it bore nothing but a Chinese ideograph.

"What's this?" said the dick, when I showed it to the others. "Did they drop it?"

Vanderhoof shrugged. "I do not know. It is perhaps a laundry ticket—we patronize the Chinese laundry around the corner. I did not see them drop it."

"Bring it along," said the dick to me. "We'll ask the interpreter about it anyhow. From the looks of that rope, it may be a Chink job, but you never can tell."

So, with the feeling that we had accomplished nothing and that the robbery would be another unsolved mystery, we went back to headquarters and interviewed the Chinatown interpreter. He glanced at the scrap of paper and laughed.

"No, it means nothing," he said. "It may be part of a laundry ticket, as the character means 'to receive'—but there's no connection with your robbery. It's not a name."

"Then good-by to them sparklers," said the dick ruefully, and handed me the torn scrap of paper. "Here's a souvenir for you— and don't forget to play up the lack of any clue. Savvy? We may drop onto something yet."

I tucked away the scrap of paper.

Lew Friedman and I usually dined together. He would rest in the late afternoon, and thus be able to sit up and work for a couple of hours in the evening, and we would read or talk together. My paper was an evening sheet, leaving me free at night.

So I brought home the robbery story, which had got into a late edition, and in the course of dinner mentioned it to Lew. That reminded me of the bit of paper, and I pulled it out.

"This may interest you—and incidentally, you may check up on that headquarters interpreter," I said, handing it to him, and telling him how the interpreter had translated the character. He glanced at it, and nodded.

"He was right—hello, though! Did it strike you that this is a queer paper for a laundryman to use? Very fine, thin rice-paper of the highest quality; I fancy it could only be procured in China or Japan. And you say the cord was partly of silk, eh? Sounds rather interesting, Dick. Let me look into it a bit after dinner."

I could not see anything to look into, but assented.

Dinner over, I wheeled Lew's chair into the big living-room and brought up his adjustable reading stand. This fixed to suit him, I got down several volumes from the wall shelves, as he indicated them. Then he chuckled.

"Go on and read your paper, now, and leave me alone. Wait! Give me that brass case on the table."

I gave him the case, which was a Chinese writing outfit— brushes, slab of ink, and water-pot. Then I lighted my pipe and settled down to read as much of my favorite author as had crept into print that day. The more I read, the more firmly convinced I became that my days as a newspaper man were numbered.

So, finally, I threw the paper aside and watched Lew. To my surprise, he seemed interested and even excited.

He was doing a good many things, too. Now he would scrape at my scrap of rice-paper with a little knife, then he would use his brush and ink on another sheet, then he would dig into one of the Chinese works I had got down for him. He was hard at work, and his big blue eyes fairly flamed, so I knew better than to ask questions; still, I began to feel the infection of his excitement, though what he could have found to interest him in that ideograph was more than I could see.

"No Chinaman ever brushed that character," he exclaimed suddenly, then relaxed and leaned back on his pillows.

"How the devil can you tell that?" I asked in surprise.

He smiled a little, and closed his eyes. He looked pallid and tired.

"Hard to say, Dick; a sort of sixth sense. The same way that an expert can rub a bronze with his hand and tell by the patina what it is; the same way a stamp collector can tell that two hinges are stuck together, though anyone else could not; the same way a rug expert can feel the wool and tell whether it's been chemically treated or not. Sense of it, that's all. I know a bit about Chinese calligraphy."

That was true enough. He knew more about it than most Chinamen do.

"Maybe you can name the man who did write it?" I asked jocularly. To my astonishment, he opened his eyes and gave me a look that went into me like steel.

"Yes—taking one thing with another, I can make a guess at it," he said slowly. "But for the love of heaven, Dick, don't go off half-cocked! Did you ever hear of a man in Pekin named Harpey? A big, brawny, intellectual Yankee who had been more years in the East than was good for him?"

"Never," I said, knocking out my pipe and reaching for my pouch.

Lew closed his eyes again and went on, "He came out as a missionary, but went into crooked ways and ended up as a pretty rich man—and he knew a lot about China. Last I heard of him, he had to leave the country in a hurry. He was a luxurious devil, always had the very best of everything, regardless of expense. Now, I haven't the shadow of a reason to connect this character with that man—except that I sense it subconsciously. That superfine paper would not necessarily point to him, neither would the fact that the ink is of the very highest quality and extremely expensive. Indeed, I don't even know that Harpey is in this country—and I hope he is not, for he is an arch criminal. But here; come over here and look. It's just possible that there is a real clue in this character."

I drew up my chair beside his. He took up a fresh sheet of paper and filled a brush with ink.

"You know that the modern Chinese writing is a contraction of the ancient writing, which consisted of pictographs," he said. "It's quite true that this character of yours means the reception of something—and it might be a laundry receipt, but it isn't. Here's the ancient character, of which it is a contraction."

He began to brush on the paper, explaining as he wrote.

"This character, *chow,* is the same used in the game of Mah Johng, with the sense of taking or receiving. Now, here is the derivation of it: The original antique character consisted of a hand giving, to another hand in a boat, taking. You'll see by this—I'll separate the component parts to make it plainer—

"At the right, a hand on the river bank passes something to another inverted hand, representing a man, in the bow of the pictograph standing for a boat. The idea is that one man on the bank gives objects to another man aboard a boat, who stows them away there. Get the picture? In the course of centuries this has been changed, little by little, and abbreviated in the course of writing, until today we have the character on your scrap of paper."

He went on to show me how successive scribes would lop off a line here or change another there; and how the original idea had come to mean merely a reception or taking, in an abstract sense. With some imagination, it was easy to see the derivation of the character. The giving hand had been changed to a symbol like an X, the receiving hand still kept its original lines, but there was nothing left of the boat except a straight line with a jag at each end.

"Well," I said, "that's all very interesting, but I don't see what it has to do with Vanderhoof's jewels."

"I don't either," said Lew, relaxing wearily. "But let's suppose. Say, for instance, that one of the robbers tore this scrap of paper off a sheet of instructions in his hurry to stow away the loot. Those instructions were carefully written in code. No ordinary Chinaman could make head or tail of them. But to one who understood that the characters were to be replaced by ancient characters—"

"I'm on, Lew!" I exclaimed. "You mean that the stuff is to be slipped aboard a boat to somebody else—when?"

"That's missing," he said, and his head drooped. "After all— it's only a wild surmise—probably nothing to it—"

The nurse happened in, took one look at Lew, and threw me out. I got my hat and went downtown. I know a hunch when I see it.

III

I CAUGHT A streetcar, and as we humped up and down hill getting to Market Street, the clue that Lew Friedman gave me looked better and better. It was logical. Not about the Harpey part, of course, but about the disposition of the stones.

They could not be disposed of in the bay cities, at least for some time; also, that character did not refer to a ferry boat—it meant too distinctly a boat, evidently. The stones would not be sent out of the country. If a gang of crooks were at work on the coast, what likelier than that stones looted in San Francisco would be sent up north to Portland or Seattle, or down south to Los Angeles, for disposition?

"Lew may have put me on a bum trail," I thought, "but it certainly looks like a hot idea to me. But how to identify the robbers?"

This question sent me to headquarters, where I found my friend the detective just going off duty. I beckoned him into the reporters' room, which was deserted at the moment, and set the whole proposition before him.

"Now," I concluded, "there were two of those birds, and they'll be sure to stick together until the loot is handed over to the third party aboard the boat. Also, they were old hands at the game—the way they pulled the job was proof of the fact. You'd stand a chance of recognizing them, while I wouldn't. Want to come in on it or not?"

The dick grinned. "Either you're wild in the head or you've got a hot clue, that's sure! I'll take no chances on gettin' the wrong kind of publicity on it. Let's you and me look up coast boats and see what we'll see. I got to get some grub, too."

I got a newspaper and we adjourned to a beanery, and looked up the coast lines. There were no boats going north until next day, but the *Golden State* was pulling out at nine that evening for San Diego.

"That's our ticket," said the detective. "We can mosey down to the pier and hang around on the quiet. There'll be a watchman and a couple o' flatties there if we need 'em."

Eight o'clock saw us at the wharf; it was a bit early, for the coast boats do not fill up until the last moment, but we were taking no chances. The reporter's badge and police star took us past the gates, and we went down the length of the warehouse where trucks were banging and stevedores shouting, to the passenger's gangway. My friend flashed his star to the officer on duty there, and we waited in the shadows. No visitors had come aboard so far, according to the officer.

Our waiting was not pleasant business, as we watched the driblets of people coming aboard—laughing women, business men, tourists. I realized clearly that the detective was losing confidence in my clue, and I myself began to think that we were on a very wild goose chase. It was a cold, foggy night and everyone was well wrapped up, but one pair in particular drew my attention—a large, elderly man of whom I could see little through his fur-lined coat except a gray beard, and the most beautiful girl I had ever laid eyes on. She wore some fur-trimmed coat that left her face framed, a perfect oval, peeping out from the setting of gray and shaggy hair, with a hint of gold beneath her fur toque and a gleaming dash of the sky in her eyes. Her eyes met mine as they passed, and for a moment I had the distinct impression of fear and anxiety, as though she were in some great peril and unhappiness. Then they were gone up the gangway, a uniformed chauffeur bringing several suitcases behind them. Millionaire tourists, I reflected, and gave my attention to the next comers. To forget the face of that girl, however, was impossible. It was like a jewel in its clear-cut beauty, and the flash of those eyes lingered with me ineradicably.

"Eight-forty," said the dick beside me. "Want to call it a day?"

"I'll quit when the gangway goes up," I said.

"All right. I'm with you—well, for the love of Mike!" He tossed away his cigarette and gripped my arm. "Look down the warehouse under that light—see 'em? Two of our best little coke peddlers and hopheads; we leave 'em to the federal squad, mostly—Whitey Jake and Chink Mose. You leave this to me, now; we got to get the evidence, that's the big thing."

"Our men," I said, peering along to where the next flaring overhead light of the warehouse showed two figures very distinctly for an instant, showed them coming toward us.

"Them birds must ha' been full of hop to pull that job today," muttered the dick. Then he left me and merged into the shadows.

You may pan the average city policeman, flatfoot or dick, all you like, but I freely admit that he knows his business when it comes to action—and I've seen more than a little of real action in my time. Those two men came along to the gangway and spoke to the officer standing there, and he motioned them up the gangway.

"Make it quick," he said. "All ashore in five minutes."

Then something happened. Those two crooks had no chance to fight, no chance to run, no chance to get rid of whatever they might be carrying. They must have thought an earthquake had struck, as my friend got a hand in each shirt-front and shook; next instant he was ironing them wrist to wrist.

"Hey! What's this for?" they demanded shrilly. "Hey, you got nothin' on us—"

"Stow the jaw," snapped the detective, and beckoned. I joined him, and we explored. In the coat pocket of my man there was a small leather wallet, strapped, and when I pulled it out we saw the name of Vanderhoof stamped across it in gold.

We had the stones.

One of the pair started to let out a shrill cry, but the dick smashed him across the lips and spoiled it.

"Now," he said to me, "go along to 102, the cabin they were asking for, and I'll be with you as quick as I can turn these birds over to the flatty out front. Savvy? We'll get the other lad while we're about it."

"Right," I said, and glanced at the ship's officer. "Number one—o—two?"

"That's the one," he said, and shrugged. "Port side, away from the wharf; a cabin de luxe. Hope you boys aren't going to keep us tied up over time?"

"Not if I can help it," I said, seeing that he took me for another dick, and with that I started up the gangway. And how

I blessed Lew Friedman in that minute! We had played a long shot and had won, incredible as it appeared!

I was mistaken in thinking the game was all over, however. The real one had not begun.

I V

FOR SOME reason or other—careless stewards, perhaps—the lights along the deck passages were not all going. Number 102 was one of the larger after cabins, and the lights were all out along that section. This, after all, was a detailed bit of planning, rather than accident, for that gang of crooks had worked things out carefully.

I had my eye on what was approximately the right cabin, and was approaching it from aft, when the door was suddenly flung open. A man, whose face I could not make out, stood for an instant in the opening.

"They have not come," he said. "I'll go to the wharf and see. Perhaps they are waiting there—the fools!"

With this he swung off up the deck, going forward. He had swung back the outer door so that it remained open; the inner door of slats was closed, light streaming through. I had no doubt that his words referred to the two crooks, but since he had obviously spoken to someone in the cabin, we had two here to deal with instead of one. So I thought it a good plan to take care of the gentleman remaining in the cabin, and leave the other for the detective.

So, immediately the departing man was out of sight and sound, I went for that slat door, and did not waste time seeing if it were locked. I put my shoulder against it and smashed the catch, and followed it inside.

"You're under arrest, so keep—" I began, then the words died on my lips. I found myself face to face with that marvelously beautiful girl whom I had seen coming aboard!

Her coat was off, and she was gowned in some dark material that set off her perfect oval of a face and her crown of golden hair. She had drawn back against the brass bed, facing me in startled alarm, yet she was not terrified out of all poise, by a long shot!

"What do you mean?" she demanded in a low voice that went through me. "Who are you? What do you want here?"

I must have looked the fool I felt in that moment.

"Beg your pardon—I got in the wrong cabin," I mumbled sheepishly. "I thought this was Number 102—"

"That's the cabin adjoining, and my uncle is occupying it," she returned. "What do you mean by saying we're under arrest?"

"Your uncle—in that number?" This was a jolt, but it braced me up like a dash of icy water. So she was a crook—this girl! "I'm sorry," I told her quickly, "but you can explain to the judge if there's a mistake. We've got the diamonds and the robbers, and—"

A spasm of wild fear crossed her face, and she swayed as though about to faint. Then she drew herself up.

"Stop, stop!" she exclaimed. "Oh, you must not—you don't understand! If he's arrested I won't have a hope left—" She broke off, then with an effort controlled herself, adding, "You're not a policeman!"

Something, some blessed impulse, impelled me to honesty.

"No, I'm not," I said, trying to figure her as I spoke. "And it's hard to believe that you're one of this gang. At the same time, I've run down this business, and the detectives will be here in a minute or two to collar your precious uncle, if they've not got him already. I'm sorry—"

"You have—you have done it?" Her eyes widened on me. "But you don't know the danger—oh, how can I explain to you! If you do this, you will suffer terribly, and they'll never let me go—you must not, you must not!"

Her words sounded incoherent, almost, hysterical, but her manner was the opposite. She impressed me as being cool enough inside, as trying to make me realize something to which I was blind. And she had twice hinted at danger to herself.

"How are you tied up with this gang?" I inquired. "My dear girl, I don't want to see you sent off to jail, I assure you, but—"

"Listen to me, listen!" she broke in rapidly, a sudden earnest imploration in her eyes. "1 can trust you, I feel it—listen to me! My uncle will never be arrested; he has friends of whom you know nothing, he has ways of reaching them—"

"Now listen to me a minute, and calm down," I said, as gently as possible. "Political pull doesn't count in this. As for his code in Chinese, I know all about it—that's why I'm here. My name is Dick Clews, and I'm on the *Star*—"

"A reporter?" She took a step forward, and impulsively seized my hand. "Listen! Let this drop for the moment—you must, if only to help me! There are two other men aboard here of whom you know nothing—they'll be here in a minute! Let me get out, please, please! For my own sake. I'll remember your name— I'll write you—send you the code, if you can read it—later on you can effect more than you can right now—"

I must confess that, at the moment, I paid little attention to her words. I thought that she wanted to get away, and wanted it desperately; and I did not blame her a bit. She was a girl of birth and breeding, if I ever saw one, and no matter how she was mixed up in this case I could not believe her a criminal.

"My dear girl," I said quietly, "if you want to go, then go. But if you'll stick it out, you can depend on me to help you to the limit, and you needn't be afraid of these—"

"I may go?" she exclaimed. I bowed slightly.

"Certainly."

She snatched up hat and cloak, and I stood aside. Hoping against hope that she would not run away, I held open the door—and without a word she darted outside and was gone.

For a moment I stood motionless, then felt a sudden realization of my utter folly in letting her cajole me. Why, she might be the head and brains of the whole gang! Her uncle, if that man with the gray beard were her uncle, might know nothing about it—

I swung open the door again, and started outside, only to come into violent collision with two men. Then, too late, I remembered what she had said about men aboard here. Too late, that is, to get in the first blow; a hard fist took me under the jaw and sent me back headfirst into the cabin, and they piled after me. To put it more correctly, they piled on me—and started to beat me up.

Neither of them was the man with the gray beard; by their attire, they were deckhands of the boat, and they fell on me tooth and nail. However, I am not exactly a baby, when it comes to taking care of myself, and in ten seconds I was on my feet and at work. I was still at work when a sharp voice broke in on us from the doorway—and there was the detective with his gun out and a flatfoot in uniform at his elbow.

The two rascals staggered to their feet.

"What's this mean?" snapped the dick. One of them pointed at me, for answer.

"We caught this feller goin' through the cabin—passenger sent us in to get him, and—"

"What passenger?" I mumbled, through swollen lips.

"Man in a fur coat, gray beard—"

"Our man!" I turned to the detective, "Didn't you get him? He went down to—"

The dick looked dazed. It appeared that he had seen nothing of the bearded man, and in two minutes we were on the way to the pier, with a whistle shrilling.

The man we were after had simply vanished. So had the girl, although I did not see fit to mention her. When we came back and searched the boat, their baggage had vanished also, and so had the two deckhands who had tackled me.

We were forced to realize the fact that we had lost the man higher up, but we had the holdup men and the diamonds. It did us no good, for they refused to talk, and nothing could draw anything from them, though Vanderhoof and his wife identified them most positively. I left myself out of the affair, and handed all the credit for the work to the detective—modestly, I thought. Had I only been able to foresee the result!

That was the way the matter ended—at least, for that night.

V

THE MORNING papers had the story, of course, but not the whole story; they gave all the credit to the detective, while I meant the *Star* to spring the sensational feature about Lew Friedman, with the human interest attaching to the way in which a hopeless cripple had brought about the capture of two bandits.

All well and good; but when, over the breakfast table, I recounted to Lew my adventure of the previous evening, and asked permission to feature him, he just sat back and stared.

"You poor fish!" he said at last. "You poor helpless fool! If you published that information about me, I'd be dead inside of two days!"

"Nonsense; and quit calling names," I said. "Here I thought you'd be astonished and grateful and a heap tickled because your tip had turned out right—instead of which you fasten your lamps on me and begin to get hysterical like that girl did!"

"Dick, your command of classic English is marvelous," he said, but just then I noticed a queer pallor about his lips, and I realized that he was fighting for self-control.

"What is it, old man?" I asked quickly. "Have I said anything to hurt—?"

He shook his head. "Don't you see, Dick? That man with the beard was Harpey, after all."

Harpey! I sat silent, staring at him, remembering what he had told me about the man away off in China. So the big man was Harpey!

"What about the girl, then?" I asked, leaning forward. "Who was she?"

"I don't know—never heard of any niece." Lew passed a hand over his eyes and spoke wearily. "Here, tell me again just what she said—her very words! Don't change 'em."

I obeyed his behest, having a very vivid recollection of the girl and her words to me. When I had finished, he nodded.

"Dick, don't you realize that the man must have been infernally clever to set those false deckhands on you, to make his own getaway, to get the girl and his luggage clear? Doesn't that give you a faint idea of his tremendous potentialities? I tell you, Dick, this man is a criminal de luxe—a criminal on a magnificent, unguessed scale! This affair of the diamonds was only a drop in the bucket."

"But the girl—"

"Worked you, to put it bluntly," said Lew, and now his eyes were flaming and glittering as I had seldom seen them; a very fire was blazing in their blue depths. "She's one of the gang, of course—"

"I don't believe it!" I exploded. "Lew, if you'd seen her face you'd know better! If it's as you think, if Harpey is really a big criminal, there's some explanation of her presence in the game. She was frightened, I tell you! And remember, she promised to let me hear from her—in code. Perhaps she serves him as secretary or something of the sort—sends out his orders without knowing what they are."

Lew's lips curved sardonically.

"Very well; we'll just wait and see if we do hear from her. But now, Dick, I'm going to be ready to fight, understand? Now I've something to live for—and I'm going to get myself in better shape. You and I are going to fight that gang!"

"Bully," I said heartily. "But I don't see any danger to you in publicity—"

"You don't? Can't you understand what sort of man this Harpey is?" he cried out. "For the love of heaven, wake up to what we're facing! You get a gun today and wear it, understand? You'll need it, I promise you. Look at the silence of those two

bandits! They'd sooner take their medicine than peach on
Harpey—why? Because they know he'd get them! They'll never
talk, even under deprivation of their drugs. Perhaps they don't
even know his name—perhaps they know him only as the man
higher up!"

His blaze of energy impressed me strangely, and gradually I
began to see the whole thing as he saw it. The conviction grew
upon me that he knew what he was talking about. And then,
suddenly, he brought down his fist on the table.

"Call up your detective friend!" he exclaimed. "Call him up
quickly, and tell him to look out for himself—if Harpey thinks
that he ran down that clue, he'll be in danger before this day is
out! Call him up here and now!"

I went to the telephone and called up headquarters, told the
sergeant who I was, and asked for the detective. The sergeant
made lengthy answer, and as I listened, I felt a cold chill steal-
ing over me. Presently I hung up the receiver and turned to
Lew.

"You're right, Lew, you're right," I said, feeling badly shaken.
"And the call was too late. As the poor chap stepped out of his
own door this morning, he was shot down by two men sitting
in an auto and waiting for him. They riddled him, and then got
away."

Lew Friedman sat back in his wheeled chair.

"Round one to Harpey," he said in a low voice. "And now—
to see if we hear from the girl!"

"We will," I said, though without conviction.

Lew smiled sardonically. "Dream on!" he said, but his voice
was a trifle sad.

11

SIERRA STREET

Strange Word Came of a Plot Concerning Sierra Street, and Dick Clews Lost No Time in Getting to the Spot; Nor Did His Plain-Clothes Sidekick—Who Was Out for Revenge

I

"**I** TELL YOU, Harpey is a menace to society!" exclaimed Lew Friedman. "I knew him well in China; he has ability plus and halts at nothing. As for that girl who calls herself his niece, she's hand and glove with him. I don't believe anything else, Clews."

"Well, I do," I retorted. "And I'm going to get her out of his clutches if I can. She's bitterly afraid of him, but she'll keep her promise to me."

For three days following the affair of the Vanderhoof diamonds, Lew Friedman had been steadily improving in health. His old spinal injury had hitherto rendered him almost helpless, but now he could sit up for several hours a day. The will of the man was at work; he was preparing to fight that arch-criminal Harpey. He had only his brain to work with, but he had me to use as the executor of his will.

Yet we were in the dark. Since our initial brush with Harpey, I had tried unavailingly to get trace of the man under whatever name he was now using. I could not rid my mind of the appealing, frightened face of that girl who called herself his niece. Her voice still rang in my ears, her beauty still thrilled me; her clear, delicate personality left me with a sense of maddened futility at not being able to reach her. I wanted to find her again, to help her, to get her clear of Harpey. She had promised to let me hear from her, had promised to send me some clue as to Harpey's activities, but nothing had come as yet.

So, on the fourth morning after the recovery of the Vanderhoof diamonds, Friedman and I had our tiff at the breakfast table; his insistence that the girl was a crook irritated me. His argument that we had not heard from her was unanswerable, but I demanded time.

"Harpey doesn't waste time," said Lew grimly. "The man is a human vulture, or better, a tiger—and tigers don't waste time. As for the girl—"

"Give her a chance, will you?" I flung at him, and departed to work.

As a newspaper reporter, I did not amount to much; but my wide acquaintance with the world, gained as a wanderer, soldier of fortune, and ex-officer in the Chinese army, let me pick up all sorts of human interest stories. While I could not read or write Chinese, I could chatter it well enough to pounce on many a good thing in Chinatown.

Due partly to my argument with Lew Friedman, and partly to my worry about the girl, whose very name I did not know, that morning found me in a black mood. Also, a big story had broken and the office was excited. One thing led to another, and at precisely eleven-thirty several things happened. The city editor got a black eye and I quit the employ of the *Star*.

I was turning in my police and fire badge and was cashing my pay check, when a copy boy brought me a letter which had just come for me—not by post, but by hand.

"A swell dame left it," he exclaimed. "She was sure in a hurry, too! Looked like she didn't want to be seen—aw, gee! Say, is this for me, honest?"

I left him staring at a five-dollar note, and hurried out. Although trembling with eagerness, I kept myself in hand until I was sitting in a streetcar and pounding out Market Street toward the western hills. Then I examined the letter, which was hurriedly addressed in pencil to Dick Clews, in care of the *Star*. Tearing it open, I found a scrap of paper on which were brushed two Chinese characters, and beneath them was scribbled in pencil: "102 Sierra Street." It all looked hastily done. I could imagine that even to get this cryptic message to me might have cost the girl untold danger.

When I reached home, Lew Friedman was resting and I had to wait impatiently until he wakened and dressed. The doctor was on hand, with a vivid interest in the recuperation of his patient, and refused to let me waken Lew. So I fretted. From the scrap of paper I could get nothing. We knew that Harpey used Chinese characters to communicate with his gang, but the peculiar code used was beyond my fathoming. It was not until an hour afterward, at luncheon, that I could tell Friedman why I was out of a job and could show him the letter.

"Don't let the job worry you," he said, glancing at the scrap of paper. "I'll stake you indefinitely, Dick. Besides, I have an idea that you may rake in some money from this fight of ours. Hm! This paper is decidedly interesting."

"Then you admit that the girl is playing straight with us!" I exclaimed exultantly.

Friedman gave me a quick look from those bright blue eyes of his, and rumpled up his mane of snowy white hair. He smiled and nodded admission.

"Yes," he stated. "She traced those two characters herself—the brushwork is extremely poor, while Harpey is a fine calligraphist. Also, this is not the expensive rice paper which we observed before. There's no doubt but that your girl serves him as secretary, and took the chance to copy these characters—"

"Why didn't she put it in English, then?" I demanded.

"Probably she doesn't know what the message means," said Lew thoughtfully. "We know that Harpey uses this code in giving orders, perhaps to some well educated Chinaman who acts as his lieutenant. If you could only see her again and get some idea where we could find Harpey—"

"Don't worry, I'd like to well enough," I said grimly. "What does this stuff mean?"

"Ah, that's another story! You'll have to wait 'til I get the glossary and trace these characters to their antique form and primitive meanings; as they stand, they make no sense."

Lew was almost as excited as I over the affair, and hurried through luncheon. Then we wheeled him into the library, the nurse adjusted his table across his knees, and I got down several books as he indicated them—all, I observed, ponderous Chinese tomes. When his brass writing-set of brushes, ink and water was in place, I drew up a chair beside him and lighted my pipe, watching him as he worked.

Perhaps ten minutes had passed, when suddenly a laugh broke from him.

"This is so simple I nearly missed it!" he exclaimed jubilantly, and took up a brush. "Look here, now! We have the two characters *Ch'ew* and *Wei;* one meaning to abuse or maltreat, the other dealing with the moon," and with swift, deft strokes he traced the two characters as they should be written.

I watched, fascinated by the magic of his brush, and awaiting the ridiculously simple explanation which was bound to come. I knew, of course, that most modern Chinese characters are abbreviations of the ancient ones, which were really pictographs, conveying ideas by means of pictures. At the same time, my mind requires charts and diagrams to see any pictures in the hen-tracks of Chinese calligraphy, and the only man I knew who could resolve this chaos into any order, was Lew Fried-

man—unless I should mention Harpey and his gang of crooks. I failed to see anything moonlike in either of the characters.

 Then Lew Friedman drew the ancient pictographs for which these stood, and there was the answer.

"We'll take *Ch'ew* first," he said. "Here's the antique form, which shows a house with pointed roof, and under it the figure of a pestle. The pestle means to pound, to abuse, to crush somebody as drugs are crushed in a mortar; hence, to maltreat or to attack somebody. Placed under a roof—"

"To attack somebody in their own house, eh?" I broke in.

"Go to the head of the class." Lew grinned at me, but he was highly excited, and his blue eyes fairly glittered. "Now look at the other figure. Here, first, is a picture of the moon rising above the horizon and still partly hidden, which stands for the beginning of the night. Add another stroke to that and you have the moon completely risen, or midnight. Then turn it around, place it on end, add a couple thousand years of re-writing, and you have the modern character. The whole message, therefore, means that Harpey's gang is to make a raid on some house at midnight. Your lady friend was probably ignorant of what was intended, but knew that it had something to do with a certain house—so she jotted down the address. And there you are!"

"There," I amended grimly, "I'll be! Hello! Buck up, Lew—"

He had overdone. The excitement under which he had labored ever since my return home, was too much for him—had burned him out. His head sagged backward, and I hurriedly called the nurse. She came in, took one look at his pallid features, and told me to beat it.

"Get out and stay out for the rest of the day," she said, "or I'll call up the doctor and get definite orders. I'm sorry, Captain Clews, but you can see for yourself—"

I went. Lew had done his part, anyway; my end of the thing was action, so I was glad to start in. Besides, I had a great little idea just about then—a really brilliant one. Such things are rare with me, but when they come, they come hard. And this was a real one.

I I

MY IDEA was simple enough, and sprang from a chance remark of Friedman's. Four days previously, the detective who helped me frustrate Harpey in our first encounter, and who got all the credit therefor, was murdered—shot down at his own door by men who escaped in their automobile. Since Harpey did not suspect that anyone else was on his trail, it was my business to see that his suspicions were not aimed at Lew Friedman, who would be all too easy a victim.

However, the plain-clothes sidekick and close friend of that murdered detective was heavyweight champion of the police force—one Terry Sullivan, a fine Mick from south of the slot. I went down, hunted him up, got him off by myself, and proceeded to tell him about the gang who had done for his friend. I told him the whole story, omitting only any mention of Lew Friedman, and made a bid for his assistance.

"If you throw in with me," I concluded, "you may or may not get the men who bumped off Jerry, but you'll sure have a crack at the gang, and it won't be any picnic either! You can't assume much credit, or you'll go the same way your pal went. You'll have to work under cover, at least until we can get hold of Harpey in person or find out who he is and where. I have nothing to go on except the occasional help from this girl—"

"Never mind all that, sir-r," broke in Terry Sullivan, half closing his eyes and giving me a cold and bitter look. "I've already got a month's leave to be runnin' down them byes that done for Jerry, and I'm wid ye from soup to nuts! As for this Harpey, we might be able to get a clue on him over at the Oakland bureau, since ye've had a sight of him."

"Then you're with me?" I asked.

"Sure. You and me are sitting in on this game, Mr. Clews, and I'm takin' orders from you, sir-r. Tell me once more, now, about this job for tonight."

I told him what we had deduced from the characters, or rather what Lew had deduced. When I mentioned the address, he gave a decisive jerk of his head.

"By the piper! That's where Reno Johnson lives."

"And who's Reno Johnson?"

He grinned at me. "You ain't a native son, eh? Reno is a big Swede who piled up a fortune in Nevada silver, back in them happy days when a bye could be stickin' his pick into the ground and pullin' it out silver-plated. Now Reno's an old nut, living all by himself in a fine house wid half a dozen Chink servants, lonely as hell and playin' politics for amusement. He's got a collection of coins, gold and silver ones, which accordin' to all reports is worth a whale o' money, but I dunno. They say that house of his is walkin' death to any cracksman. Our friend Harpey would think twice about tacklin' it."

I laughed. "We're not up against boys from the Mission, Sullivan! If Johnson has Chinese servants, then it's an inside job; we believe that Harpey's lieutenant is a Chink. But this is more than mere robbery. That first Chinese character stood for bodily assault. Has this man Johnson any enemies?"

"Nothin' but, sir-r!" said Sullivan. "As ye'd know if you'd been born and bred here. Whisper, now—the politicians and the City Hall crowd would call it a public holiday if he was bumped off! He's one of these here pure politics cranks, besides which he hates all the world; and them byes always gets hated in return, take it from me. Likely this gang would be killin' two birds wid one blackjack—puttin' him out of the way and grabbing the money, too."

"Likely enough," I assented. "Where and when shall we meet tonight?"

"A block below his house—the California Street cable will take ye close by—at eleven-thirty. I'll drop in at the precinct station and be tellin' the flatty who has that beat to keep his ears open for a whistle. We'll see what turns up."

"Right," I said. "Now, I want a permit to carry a gun. Can you help me there?"

"Sure thing, sir-r! We'll tend to that here and now," said he, and we did.

I did not return home that afternoon or evening, because I knew that the nurse meant exactly what she said. Lew Friedman had plenty of money and got the best he could get; and the best in trained nurses not only comes high but rules with a firm hand. So, instead of going home, I betook myself to the Ferry Building and went over to Oakland.

There I made extensive inquiries at the famous police head-quarters, having had a glimpse of Harpey myself and knowing him also from Lew Friedman's description. The only result was a large waste of time, for I got not the slightest clue as to Harpey's present identity. So I came back to town, recklessly squandered my money on a good dinner, and then went to a movie in the company of a good cigar. Those big, easy balcony chairs and the ability to smoke while you look both make for comfort and relaxation.

So, feeling better, at eleven o'clock I walked down to the turntable at the foot of California Street, boarded one of the absurd little cable cars, and settled down for my cold night ride to the western heights. It was not only cold, but quite foggy.

I had previously considered going to Reno Johnson myself, but had decided against this course. First, whoever was on the inside of the job would probably take warning; and second, Johnson himself was not the sort of person to tamper with. He was old, irascible, full of notions, and would probably be very suspicious. In the third place, I was a trifle nervous about Lew Friedman's deductions, and about the information itself. The best plan was to keep an eye on the place and see if our tip worked out aright.

It was just eleven-thirty when I got off the car, lighted my pipe, and started up the steep hill. Sierra Street was dark and deserted and clammy with fog. This was one of the sections of the city still lighted with antique gas lamps, and it had also escaped the big fire; the houses were gloomy old piles, once handsome Victorian residences, and due to the site each one stood well above the sidewalk.

A dark figure loomed ahead at the appointed corner, and I recognized Sullivan. He gave me a curt word of greeting, as I knocked out my pipe.

"Know the place? Come along, I'll show you."

In three minutes he was pointing out the house—a large structure to which one ascended by a score of steps. The house was unlighted. Everyone was asleep, apparently.

"Better get out of the street, sir-r," said he, and motioned upward. "Right forninst the buildin' itself is a good place to be waitin'. If you'll watch the front, I'll be keepin' me eye on the back—no tellin' which way they'll come."

"Right."

We silently ascended the steps; it was impossible to make out anything distinctly for the fog and darkness. Sullivan vanished, and I drew in against one end of a large veranda. There I settled down to wait.

The time dragged interminably. An occasional belated pedestrian wakened echoes with faint footfalls, but nothing else happened. I reflected that the time indicated by that lunar character was none too definite—we might have to wait here for hours. The possibility was chilling to contemplate.

Ah!

A squeak of brakes, a slight jar, and peering down at the street I made out a shadowy mass; a car had come down the hill, coasting silently, and had stopped before the house, no lights showing. I slipped quietly around the side of the house, and almost collided with Terry Sullivan.

"They're here," I told him, and we retraced our way to the front. Hugging close to the house, we waited. A brief murmur of voices, then silent figures appeared mounting the steps—two men, no more. A flashlight darted a swift gleam to the sidewalk, then from the dark veranda above came a low word.

Sullivan tensed; the same thought struck us both—had that inside worker on the veranda, who was evidently opening the house to the two bandits, discerned us? Obviously not, for the two mounted to the veranda, and we caught a low laugh, a cruel and deadly sound.

"Follow 'em," I breathed to Sullivan. "Close behind or we lose."

We took a step or two, and saw the electric torch leap out and illumine an opened window, beside which stood a third figure; for an instant we had sight of an Oriental face, a dark Chinese costume, then all was blackness again. There was a slight scuffle as the three men entered the opening, then silence.

I led the way, for it was imperative that we take the risk of following them closely, since we dared not use any light and did not know the interior of the place or their objective. Gaining the veranda and leaving Sullivan to follow at will, I slipped to the window and entered without trouble. As I did so, another flash of light gleamed on the opposite side of the large room, and showed a doorway and hall into which the three were going.

Not daring to follow too closely, I was at the doorway a moment later. All sign of the three had now disappeared; the hall was dark and empty. Moving forward cautiously, I waited, then discerned a faint glimmer of light from beneath a door which was closed. Going to the door, I gripped the handle and turned cautiously; the door opened toward me, and next instant I stood in the same room with the three.

It was a large room, heavily adorned with objects of art. The electric torch was now burning steadily, its ray of light fastened upon the opposite wall, and the reflected gleam allowed me to perceive a good deal. The three men stood around a glass-topped table against the wall. Above this table hung a large panel of Chinese tapestry, which the saffron servant was holding back. The torch ray fell upon the face of a large glass case built into the wall, and showed the glitter of coins. There before us was the best of Reno Johnson's numismatic collection—coins worth thousands of dollars each.

The three men now conferred for a moment. Having no idea where Sullivan was, I took the opportunity to slip behind a large upholstered chair and crouch there, watching.

"Go ahead," said one of the two intruders, with a soft laugh. "Give us ten minutes here, then bring him down. Sure these are the keys? All right."

The Chinese servant slipped away and was gone at once. The two cracksmen ripped down the priceless tapestry hanging and gave their attention to the wall case, which was divided into several compartments. It was obvious that the servant had given them the keys, for in two minutes they had the cases wide open.

The beautifully smooth and perfect manner in which the job was being handled, evidenced Harpey's diabolical certainty. Neither of these two men was Harpey. I had a vivid memory of him as a large, burly man with leonine head and gray beard, while these two were smaller and more deadly persons. The Chinaman had gone to waken Reno Johnson and apprise him that thieves were in the house—and to bring him to his fate.

So was proven the marvelous correctness of Lew Friedman's reading—that cryptic two-character message had not lied! Harpey was combining business with pleasure. Reno Johnson would be murdered, and the blame would fall upon those who looted his collection; it would never be guessed that the real object of the raid was the premeditated murder of the man in his own house! And Harpey would make a big haul from those coins. The torch ray swept to the glass top of the table, and was reflected from the gold and silver coins that began to fall upon it.

III

THE TWO cracksmen experienced some difficulty in prying loose the coins from their velvet setting, and did not hesitate to use force. One by one, the bits of gold and silver clinked on the glass top of the table. Then, suddenly, I had a swift and clear-cut vision of one man's face as he turned to the safe in the light of the electric torch, and I knew him.

The man was John Li or Lee—an American born Chinaman, very highly educated, who had gone to the bad. Six months previously he had gone to San Quentin, a convicted murderer. Within two days he had escaped, and pictures of him were now plastered all over the state, with a reward of two thousand upon him alive or dead. He had completely vanished—and here he was!

In a flash, I knew that we had solved one mystery. Here was Harpey's lieutenant, the man to whom those cipher messages were sent—the one man in a thousand who could understand them!

"That's enough," said John Lee, and laughed softly. It was the same deadly laugh I had heard outside, with a steely ring to it. "We can't take all, you fool—they must think that he disturbed us at the job—"

The other man growled, and reluctantly desisted from his work. John Lee spread out a handkerchief and began to make a bundle of half the coins lying on the table.

"Remember now," he said softly, "remember how it's to be done—"

"I'm sick o' you and your damned Chink ways," snapped the other man viciously. "There's no sense to the whole scheme, like I told you."

"Well," returned Lee, "you'd better bear in mind what—"

I jumped. There came a click, and the room was flooded with electric light. The two men whirled about, so completely surprised that they had not time to reach for a weapon.

"Put 'em up!" snapped a metallic voice—certainly not that of Sullivan. I twisted a little farther around the chair to see the speaker.

It was Reno Johnson, clad in a dressing-gown over his pajamas and holding a big forty-five on the two cracksmen as he stood in the farther doorway. He was a harsh-featured, wrinkled old man, but looked as though he meant business—which he did. The two cracksmen swiftly elevated their hands.

I had my pistol ready, thinking that they intended to shoot Johnson as he came upon them; their more clever game did not penetrate my thick skull at all. Then, just behind Johnson, appeared the yellow servant who had wakened and brought him here. I saw the saffron hand leap out with a flash of steel. It was to be noiseless—deadly—the blame cast upon the escaped cracksmen.

The horror of it paralyzed me, nor could I fire without hitting Johnson. I cried out frantically; the cry was drowned in the blast of a shot just behind me. The traitorous servant pitched forward past Johnson and fell into the room, his knife flying afar as he died. I glanced around to see Sullivan, a police whistle shrilling from his lips.

I rose from behind my chair, tasting momentary triumph. Ecstatic realization of a dozen things shot through my brain— all the while Sullivan's whistle was screeching. We had those two cracksmen where we wanted them. There was no love lost between them, and from what I had overheard, the second man would peach readily on John Lee and Harpey. Indeed, he was a little rat-faced rascal, gaping at us in stark fright, while Lee stood in frozen silence. Then, indeed, we had everything in our hands, the whole game won at a blow!

We had forgotten Reno Johnson.

He, not aware of what was behind all this business, not yet alive to the black treachery of his servant, thought that we were two more members of the gang who had shot down his faithful houseboy. He supposed that our guns were meant for him.

Abruptly, bravely, he lunged at the electric switch, threw the room into darkness, and opened fire. It was all done in an instant, before Sullivan's whistle blast was finished. The room became an inferno. The electric torch, lying on the table, played its pallid beams over the wall. The red jets from Johnson's revolver split the darkness. Then the rest of us were involved in the tumult and confusion—I shooting for John Lee, while Sullivan cursed and crashed to the floor as Johnson's bullets reached him. It was a tragic and horrible debacle.

Realizing that Sullivan was down, I turned and flung for the doorway, only to collide with a figure; we came together full tilt. It was John Lee, too crafty to use a pistol, now seeking only escape. A slung shot caught me glancingly, dazing me, and a second blow struck my hand and knocked my pistol away. I landed a wild swing, felt my fist crunch home, heard the man grunt as my knuckles smashed on lips and teeth. Then he was gone.

Remembering the waiting car, I darted into the hall. A door slammed—Lee was ahead of me. With a curse at the loss of my pistol, I was after him, only to gain the outer room an instant too late. Rushing to the open window, I scrambled out, with a glimpse of his figure vanishing in the obscurity ahead. The policeman from the beat was hammering at the door, but quite failed to see either of us as we emerged at the far side of the veranda. I did not pause to instruct him, but hurled on down the steps toward the street below.

Lee was not ten feet ahead of me, and from the head of the street-stairs I took a flying leap. One hundred and ninety pounds of Dick Clews came down squarely on his neck—and both of us were hurled headfirst into the car waiting at the curb. It was a grand smash, but a sad one for me; my head struck the unyielding edge of the running-board, causing an inch-long gash in the scalp and laying me out for half a minute. That half-minute was all John Lee needed. He was hurt, but somehow scrambled into the tonneau of the car.

I staggered up to hear the engine soar into life—and realized that another person had been left in the car. Gears clashed and meshed; I reeled forward, made the running-board, and reached madly in at the figure behind the wheel. Then the dashlight flashed on, and with a cry of astounded wonder and incredulity, I lost my grip as the car jerked ahead and flung me. Landing on the sidewalk, I rolled over and came to my feet to see a red tail-light vanishing down the hill.

The face behind the wheel still held me dumbfounded. It was the face of the unknown girl who called herself Harpey's niece—the girl who had sent me the tip! It was she who was driving the car!

IV

I WAS STILL numbed by the sight of that girl's face, as I stumbled back up to the house. My supposition had been that she was somehow held under the thumb of that terrible man Harpey, whom she called her uncle; but I had never dreamed that she took any active part in his depredations on society. Why she should do so remained a mystery, which I could only accept in the hope that time would clear it up; the fact that she had been out in that car all the while, that I might have seen her and talked to her, left me all staggered.

So, in a more physical sense, did the handsome little scalp-cut that I had received. When I got up to the house, I was a pretty sight. The servants were up and being herded into one room by the uniformed policeman, while to my great relief I found . Terry Sullivan still alive and only slightly scraped by the bullet; he was just reaching an explanation with Reno Johnson, who by this time comprehended the situation fairly well, or at least the salient aspects of it.

"I may have made a mess of it," said old Reno grimly, "but how the devil was I to know who you were? Your own fault for not showing your star—"

"Expect me to be flashin' a star and blowin' a whistle and holdin' down a gun on a bird like John Lee all to wanst?" began Sullivan heatedly. "Praise be, it's lucky you are—"

"Cut out the argument, gentlemen," I broke in. Johnson turned and surveyed me.

"Who's this, and what have you got there?"

Sullivan told him that I was responsible for the evening's enjoyment.

"I've got a fine little cut over the head," I said to Johnson, "and that scoundrel Lee got clear away in their car—"

"But what's that in your fist, sir-r?" demanded Sullivan, grinning suddenly.

I looked down, and found a little forgotten bundle in my fingers. I had picked it up after colliding with Lee and the automobile together, and had clung to it subconsciously. It was the handkerchief-knotted loot.

"That's your collection of coins, or what they took of it," I said, and handed over the precious little bundle to Johnson. "Where's the second crook who was here?"

Sullivan stepped to one side, revealing the second cracksman. He lay outstretched with a blue mark in the center of his forehead—a bullet had fixed him. It had helped to fix us, too; Sullivan gave me a grim look, and I knew that the same idea was in both our minds. We had bungled a great chance—just how great, I alone knew. I was not minded to tell anyone who had driven that car.

Now it was necessary to get away, however, so I turned to Reno Johnson. He was pawing over the coins in the bundle.

"We don't want to show up in this," I said. "We'll leave that bull in the next room to take the credit and make his report."

"Wait!" said Johnson, and flung a look at the sprawled body of his treacherous servant. "Wait! What was behind this? Plain robbery—or the other thing?"

"The other thing," I said, meeting his keen old eyes. "But it must be made to appear a simple robbery, frustrated by the devotion of your faithful servant, who paid with his life for the deed."

"You damned sardonic beggar!" he broke in, with a grim laugh. "So that's it, eh? Very well. Now, you two—I owe you a lot more than money can pay; but you've saved some mighty precious coins tonight. If you ever need a friend, come to me. Meantime, take these to remember me by. Good thing nobody knew I had 'em here—"

He pulled out a drawer in the glass-topped table, and the electric light scintillated on a jeweler's box containing some cut but unset stones—diamonds, and big ones. He pressed two of them into my hand, others into Sullivan's ready paw. I started to protest, but swallowed my pride. Why not? I was practically broke and out of a job, I had paid with skin and bone for the night's work, and Johnson could certainly afford to pay for what we had saved him. So, slipping quietly away, Sullivan and I melted into the night.

"Glory be!" When we were walking down the steep street in the fog, Sullivan exhaled a long breath. "Glory be, but we got one o' them byes that done for poor Jerry! And the other was John Lee, with two thousand on his head—"

"He's more than just that," I said morosely. "He's Harpey's chief lieutenant, who carries out the jobs that Harpey frames up for him."

Sullivan whistled. "Then we've bungled it, and no mistake!"

We had. Between this reflection, and the memory of the girl in the car, I was not in a happy frame of mind as I went home to tell Lew Friedman what the moon-at-midnight character had meant. As Terry Sullivan said, we had only one hope, which was no consolation at all.

Better luck next time!

III

THE HOUSE ON THE DUNES

*The Brixton Robbery and Murder Case Was
a Celebrated One in Police Circles of the
Pacific Coast, and The Way It Tied Up With
Other Crimes Would Have Been a Mystery
Had It Not Been for Young Dick Clews*

TERRY SULLIVAN, on leave from headquarters, came up to our house in Millard Street, the same morning we heard from the unknown girl. Two days had passed uneventfully since the moon-at-midnight affair.

I brought Sullivan into the library and introduced him to Lew Friedman, explaining that Lew was almost hopelessly crippled by an old spinal injury, could only sit up for an hour or two at a time, and was the Chinese scholar who had interpreted the cryptic messages sent by Harpey to his crook lieutenant. Sullivan lighted a cigar and made himself comfortable.

"We know this much," he said. "John Lee is head of the gang under Harpey, and that Chink crook had a life sentence on him when he escaped from San Quentin. He's a bad man, sir-r, and I'm thinkin' we'll be puttin' a bullet into him next time and talkin' afterward. Have ye heard no more from the young lady, Mr. Clews?"

"No," I said, frowning. "Sit down and talk it over with Mr. Friedman, while I run down the street and get some tobacco, will you? I'm clear out. Tell him about Harpey, Lew, and the man's record in China. Back in five minutes."

I left the house and descended the steep hill-street, one of the many in San Francisco which a car can scarcely climb. I had only two blocks to go, dropped in at my usual cigar store, and got some tobacco. I stood a moment at the curb to fill my pipe, when an automobile suddenly swerved in beside me and

halted with a scream of brakes. The driver was a girl—my girl—
the unknown girl who called herself Harpey's niece!

She was alone in the car, was thrusting an envelope at me,
while I stood stupefied by this unexpected meeting. It was pure
chance, of course—

"Quickly—take it!" she cried. "I was going to mail it—tried
to yesterday and had no chance. I don't know what it means. It
has something to do with the Brixton case—"

I seized the envelope, leaped to the running board and got
a grip as she threw in the gears. I had one flashing glimpse of
her face, so delicate and rarely beautiful.

"Wait!" I exclaimed. "You must wait—your name—where I
can find you—"

"You can't. I'm Claire Maynard. Get off, get off! It's dangerous."

She was whipping right up into speed. I swiftly gave her
Lew Friedman's address, since I was without a job and she could
not reach me at the newspaper office.

"For my sake—get off!" she cried, her face desperate. "I may
be watched—"

At this plea I jumped; it was not unlikely that she was spied
upon. I did not even know her position in Harpey's gang, except
that she was compelled to share in some of their actions, and
stood in terrible fear of her uncle. Yet she did not seem the type
of girl to yield easily to mere physical terror.

So I leaped. Staggered as I was by the unexpected meeting, I still had some brains left; and as the car whirled away, I got its license number.

Five minutes afterward I burst in upon Friedman and Sullivan with my news. The headquarters man whipped out a pencil.

"Praise be, sir-r, give me that number! Sure you got it right?"

"Right," I exclaimed. "And now we'll find where Harpey lives."

Lew Friedman only smiled thinly and lay back in his wheeled chair. I gave him the envelope.

"Do you really think so?" he said. "Harpey is too old a bird to be caught that way, but go ahead. Don't miss any chances. So this message is connected with the Brixton case, eh?"

He regarded the envelope with a tantalizing deliberation, knowing that I was on tenterhooks to read the message. So, for that matter, was the detective, particularly at mention of the Brixton case. None of us had associated that affair with Harpey. There was no reason to do so, since the actual criminal was known—or so it was considered.

The story had broken only the day previous; a particularly atrocious crime. Brixton, a retired Eastern banker, who lived near Monterey, had motored up to San Francisco and had bought some very handsome jewels for his wife; he had also drawn a large sum in cash, and had then started for home, taking money and jewels with him. His body had been found during the previous afternoon on the coast highway not five miles south of San Francisco; he had been shot from behind and robbed. The chauffeur and car had vanished. It was a plain case of murder, and the chauffeur was being hunted throughout the state; he was a man named Redtree, and was said to be badly in need of money. There was nothing to connect this crime with any of Harpey's gang; nothing, that is, on the surface.

But now Lew Friedman opened the letter and drew out a sheet of paper on which were two brushed ideographs. He examined them swiftly, critically.

"That's the girl's writing!" he exclaimed. "It's poorly done, while Harpey is a beautiful calligraphist. She has copied a message sent Lee—yesterday, you say?"

"She said she had tried to mail it yesterday and failed, or I inferred as much," I said.

"Then we have here the instructions sent Lee," said Lew Friedman musingly, while Sullivan stared from the ideographs to his white-haired, ascetic head in astonished awe that any man could understand such writing. "Undoubtedly, Harpey and Lee agree on certain alternative schemes or  plans, and at the last minute Harpey sends his lieutenant instructions on which plan to follow. Yet I don't make sense from these characters. The first is *Yinn*, meaning an argument or reason; the second seems to be *Ch'ou*, or cedar. Hm!"

Then we fell to work. Sullivan went to the telephone and called headquarters, putting in a request for information regarding the automobile license number, while I got Lew settled with a table adjusted across his wheelchair, and then reached him down the Gloss and other big Chinese tomes from the bookshelves that lined the room.

Presently he requested the brass writing outfit, and I got it for him, filling the water-pot with fresh water. He seized a brush and began to trace out characters rapidly. A ring came at the telephone, and Sullivan answered. He hung up again, with a disgusted oath.

"They say there's no such license number—glory be, what fools them byes are."

"No such thing," and Lew Friedman looked up, a slight smile touching his lips. "Didn't I tell you that you'd never catch Harpey that way? He makes his own license plates, that's all."

Sullivan looked at me and grimaced. Lew Friedman looked down at his paper and frowned.

"Can't you make it?" I asked. He shrugged.

"Oh, yes—but to get Harpey's exact meaning is another thing. Here y'are, now."

Lew himself was a beautiful calligraphist. His years in China, his deep study of the written language, had made him expert with the brush.

"Here are the ancient characters," and he pointed to the first he had traced. "The figure of an adult man enclosed in a circle; that is, a man shut up or confined. Today it's used in the sense of argument, or that with which a man is enclosed in a verbal sense. I take it to mean that Harpey ordered a certain man taken and put in a safe place. So much for *Yinn*. The other character is not so simple and has been more altered by modern scribes.

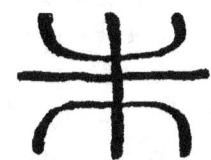

"Here is the ancient figure of a tree—a picture of the object, with its branches in the air and its roots in the ground. But across the center of it is drawn a line, to indicate that here it's a question of the center of the tree, the trunk. This is the conventional character for a tree with a red trunk or center, such as a cedar—"

"Redtree, glory be!" exclaimed Sullivan, drawing in his breath sharply. "That chauffeur in the Brixton case!"

So it looked to me, too, but Lew Friedman shook his head.

"I don't think so." He leaned back on his pillows, tiring rapidly from the concentration of his work. His face began to look pallid, a sure sign that he had overdone. "I don't think so. Lee must have known with whom he had to deal. Harpey would not have used such a character to indicate the chauffeur, though it is a temptation to call it such, in view of the chap's name of Redtree. We must look further."

A sudden thought struck me, "What's the general idea, then? That the chauffeur is to be shut up somewhere—that Harpey is behind this crime? Then—"

"By the poker, it was that murderer Lee done it!" cried out Sullivan. "They done it and carried off the chauffeur! Mr. Friedman, sir-r, it's a grand head ye have, and you a sick man with it all! Lee managed it, so the chauffeur would be blamed for the killing!"

Lew closed his eyes and nodded assent. But I had not finished.

"Hold on, now, Sullivan! We'll suppose that this is Harpey's doing—but what next? That second character would not stand for Redtree, as Lew says—there would be no point in Harpey sending such a message to his lieutenant. We'll suppose that the first scheme was to kill the chauffeur, or carry him off, and Harpey was not quite certain about where to put him. He sends word to Lee in regard to this part of the job, and Lee carries it out. Then what would that second character mean? Where Redtree was to be kept confined, naturally."

"Right," murmured Lew faintly. Sullivan looked at me and nodded, his eyes keen.

"And where did the murder take place?" I went on. "Down the peninsula, not five miles out of town, in the very heart of the heavy-traffic section, in broad daylight; Then what? The car, we'll say, was made away with. Where was the chauffeur taken? Now, if you'll recall, there's a branch road crosses the highway close to the murder scene, and goes off toward Halfmoon Bay and the coast. There's a resort section along there, a little clump of fine bungalows and cottages, by the name of Redwood Bluff—"

"Glory be, you've hit it!" sang out Sullivan exultantly. Then he sprang to his feet and leaned forward. "Here, give him a hand, quick."

Lew's head had fallen sideways on the pillows. He had gone to pieces.

II

IT SEEMED absurd to Sullivan that so much could be read in two Chinese characters, but he was quick to sense the value of the clue and the code used. Changed and abbreviated by scribes through several thousand years, the modern characters had neither the appearance nor the meaning of the ancient ones, but when traced down by Lew Friedman's keen brain, they gave us exactly what we most needed to know.

"The first thing is to locate which place in Redwood Bluff they're using," I told Sullivan. We were on a street car, heading downtown, for the nurse had taken charge of Friedman and had promptly ordered us out of the house.

"You'd better go down there and investigate," I said. "Redtree is in no danger. Harpey is undoubtedly keeping him there a few days, and then will arrange to have him nabbed with some of the loot in his possession—send him away drunk or doped. The chauffeur would never have a chance to be acquitted."

"Never a chance, sir-r," agreed Sullivan, and rose as we came into Market Street. "I'll be on my way, then, Mr. Clews; I can get a stage along here anywheres. So long, sir-r!"

He swung away. Big Terry Sullivan had a quarrel of his own with Harpey's gang, who had shot down his side-kick in cold-blooded murder, and he was on leave with the object of getting the killers. He got one of them when we saved Reno Johnson's life and coin collection from the gang, and in consequence Sullivan could have about anything he wanted from headquarters.

We had learned things, too. Harpey was still a mystery, but we knew that his chief lieutenant, the man who carried out his plans, was one John Lee, a highly educated Chinese of American birth, a half-caste. Lee was a murderer, had escaped some time previously from San Quentin, and there was a large reward for him dead or alive. Harpey was shielding him and making use of him with an infernal craft.

If Harpey ever suspected that Lew Friedman was reading his code, he would murder that helpless man in a moment. If he suspected that Sullivan and I were interfering with him, he would be after us no less quickly. If he suspected that Claire Maynard were helping us, were sending us his messages which she herself did not understand, I shuddered to think of her fate. Thus far, he had no reason to suspect any of us, but it was no wonder that she had implored me to leave her quickly after that chance meeting of this morning!

I stayed on the car to the Ferry Building, and as it swung around the circle, dropped off. My plans were nil; I could only hang around and await word from Sullivan, which would hardly come before late afternoon. I was well fixed for money, as the Reno Johnson affair had paid us handsomely; making money by baulking Harpey was not a very healthy occupation, however.

Barely had I touched the ground, when I heard my name called, and looked around to see Zimmerman beckoning me into the arcade. We had known each other in China, where he was rewrite man for the Tientsin *Times* while I was serving as an officer in the Chinese army; and when I struck San Francisco broke, he got me a job on the *Star,* for which sheet he was the leading news sleuth.

"What you doing now, Dick?" he demanded.

"Spending my income. Aren't you off your beat down here?"

"Not me. I'm watching for that Brixton case chauffeur—I've got a hunch he might try the Oakland ferry. Every bull and dick that's loose is keeping his eyes peeled. Brixton's widow has offered ten thousand reward for the chauffeur. Did your big friend find you?"

"What big friend?" I said, thinking more about that offered reward.

"Shaefer, the chap with whiskers, who knew you in Pekin."

I looked at him hard. "Who? I don't know any Shaefer, except that Dutchman who had the brewery up beyond Tientsin. What are you talking about, anyhow?"

"Fellow breezed into the office yesterday," said Zimmerman, "and they steered him onto me. He claimed he knew you in Pekin, wanted to know if you were on the paper now, and where you lived. To tell you the truth, I didn't like the way he talked—"

I went cold suddenly. "What did he look like?" I said quickly.

"Six foot two or three, grizzled whiskers, a big fur coat."

"My Lord!" I said, and swallowed hard. It was Harpey himself—on my trail!

"What's the matter?" said Zimmerman, eyeing me keenly. "Friend of yours?"

"No," I said. "Did you tell him my address?"

"Not me. I sent him down the Mission looking for you. Told him you'd had a scrap with the C.E. and quit. Who's the old boy, anyhow?"

For a minute I could only draw deep breaths of relief—not for my own sake, so much as for that of Lew Friedman. Then I took Zimmerman's arm and led him out of the crowd.

"Zimmy," I said, "that was the bird who killed Brixton."

"Hm! You don't look drunk," he grunted. "Out to Jake Clary's place last night?"

"Forget it," I told him. "That was the man behind the killing, anyhow. As for that chauffeur, Redtree, you'll never find him around here. He's down the peninsula."

"Go on, spill it," he said, suddenly cool and earnest.

"I can't do it, Zimmy," I said. "But I'll arrange to give you the break of the story."

"Right."

"And if you ever lamp that whiskered chap again, grab him. He's Harpey—"

"Jumping jingoes! Harpey, who was kicked out of China?" exclaimed Zimmerman.

"Yes, and keep it dark. Don't dare mention him in any story, if you value your life! Get him first and talk later. You can go on back to work and forget the Redtree reward—I'm after that myself."

"Damn the reward! I want the story," he said quickly.

"Then call me up at seven tonight," and I gave him Friedman's telephone number, then left him staring after me and walked away.

Harpey after me! There could be no doubt of it, and it was paralyzing news. If Harpey ever dropped onto poor Lew Friedman, who was clinging to life by a slender enough thread, that thread would be snapped in a moment. Lew had cautioned me enough. But why was Harpey after me?

Probably, I reflected, Harpey had been given a hint by Lee. That rascal Lee might have known me by sight. I had all but caught Lee the night of the Johnson affair, and he might have seen me. To a man of Harpey's diabolic cleverness and ingenuity, it would not be hard to discover that I had been working for the *Star*, and Harpey might have known of me in China.

I hunted up a friend and got a drink. I needed it.

III

I DID NOT see Lew until dinner, when the nurse wheeled him in to the table. Then I told him what had taken place, and what I had heard from Zimmerman. A flame leaped into his blue eyes, and for a moment his lips were compressed.

"We knew what we were going up against, that's all," he said quietly. "Heard from Sullivan?"

"No."

He made no further reference to the matter. It was getting on to seven o'clock when the telephone rang, and the nurse summoned me into the library to answer a long-distance call. It was Sullivan, somewhere down the peninsula.

"All right, sir-r," he said, hearing my voice. "I've got 'em spotted. Cap'n O'Brien and two of the byes will be around for you in a few minutes wid a headquarters car. You're to pick me up where the Redwood Bluff road leaves the boulevard."

"Is Harpey there?" I asked.

"I dunno. Ain't seen anyone to answer his description. And for the love of the saints, will ye be bringin' me somethin' to eat? There's no restaurants anywheres here, nothin' but millionaires' palaces."

"Sure," I said, and he rang off. I was still reporting to Lew Friedman, when my friend Zimmerman rang up. I told him to go to headquarters in an hour and stick around there until Captain O'Brien came back, and he would get the story. Then I hung up.

"There's a chance that you'll nab Harpey," said Lew. "Don't forget your gun."

"No danger," I said, and cocked my head to listen as a car roared up the hill on low. "There they are. So long, Lew."

"Good luck to you, Dick," he said, and it was a fervent utterance.

Ten minutes later, we were over Twin Peaks and whining along the coast highway at fifty miles an hour. In the car were O'Brien, the police captain, with his chauffeur and two plainclothes bulls. Nobody said very much. O'Brien had taken his orders from Sullivan, and was not sure whether to resent the fact or not; if nothing showed up at the end of the run, Sullivan would catch it. If something did show up, the big dick would get his chevrons. And O'Brien did not know where I came in. He thought I was a newspaper man who had tipped off Sullivan. He did not like it a bit, and consequently he was determined to ignore me. This, of course, suited me down to the ground. I wanted no publicity.

We were not long in reaching the turnout where Sullivan awaited us. When the car stopped, he climbed in and seized the two sandwiches I handed him.

"Come on, now!" growled O'Brien, who was from the south of the slot himself. "Ye say that ye got Redwood, ye big stiff? Then where is he and why ain't ye got him?"

Sullivan grinned happily. "He's in a bungalow over by the shore, sir-r. A brand new house it is, all by itself in the sand, praise be! But he ain't the lad that pulled the thrick, sir-r—it was John Lee. Lee is there keepin' him prisoner, Lee and two of his pals."

"John Lee!" broke from O'Brien. "You're sure of this?"

"I seen him meself, sir-r, drivin' up in a car and goin' into the house. He's there now."

O'Brien, who was sitting in front, told the chauffeur to go ahead, and we swirled out on the road toward the coast. Sullivan, gulping the last of his bread and meat, squatted down in the tonneau by me. I breathed a word in his ear.

"Harpey?"

"Divil a sign of him. Nobody there but Chinks."

That dashed my hopes. I had been steadfastly counting upon catching Harpey with the gang; but now I realized what we might have seen earlier. Harpey was not mixed up with Lee's men, from the very fact that he was sending them instructions. Lee was the doer; Harpey was the crafty planner of every stroke, keeping himself clear. And unless we actually caught Harpey we would never implicate him. None of his men would talk— perhaps none except Lee knew him or was aware of his connection.

Sullivan told the captain, as we rode, our outline of the crime as it must have been actually committed. Then, mindful of the warnings that had been impressed upon him, and mindful likewise of O'Brien's glum silence, he continued craftily:

"Please, sir-r, I'll not be wantin' any publicity in this here business. I hear tell that a reward's been offered; that'll be all right betwixt me and Mr. Clews, but we don't want to be gettin' our names in the papers, sir-r. Some o' them byes is the ones that done for poor Jerry, and if so be we don't land the whole gang, I'll keep afther 'em."

O'Brien was more than a little delighted at this delicate intimation that the public credit for the business might go to him.

"If it's as you say, Sullivan," he said, "you'll be a sergeant tomorrow; the reward goes to you, anyhow."

A sharp word broke from Sullivan—we had gone far enough in the car. The chauffeur drew up and switched off his lights, then all six of us piled out. The night was dark, with fog boding.

The thunder of the surf along the shore filled the darkness. This was a newly opened section, with streets laid and a few sidewalks in, but fewer houses; the bungalows were little more than summer cottages belonging to semi-affluent people. Not many of them were now occupied. Sullivan led us toward the glimmer of a light which shone between the street-way and the sandy beach—the bungalow in question was built squarely on the dunes, without a tree around it. About the house and the presumable lot on which it was built, Sullivan told us, there ran a fence of light palings. An automobile stood in the street before the house, a small car without lights. It was the one in which John Lee had arrived.

"All right," said O'Brien, and took charge. He told me curtly enough to stay where I was. "You come along with me, Sullivan, The other three circle around the house and watch the back."

I made no objections as the other men melted away in the darkness toward the black mass of the house ahead. It was only three nights since I had encountered John Lee in the flesh. I was still hurt and bruised from that encounter, and I was entirely willing that O'Brien should bear the brunt of this one, particularly as he would get the credit.

Not that I had any idea of staying where I was, however. The others gone, I went straight to the silent car standing in the new-built street. Remembering the way Lee had got away from us before, remembering how Claire Maynard had acted that night as chauffeur for the gang, I wondered if she were sitting in the car now—perhaps it was the same one she had been driving this morning!

On approaching the car cautiously, however, I found it quite empty. Stooping above the front license plate, I fingered the raised numbers and discovered that this was not the car the girl had driven in the morning; it was a smaller machine, of cheaper make.

"The chances are that she's not here," was my thought, "and has nothing to do with this affair. Sullivan would have mentioned it had he seen her, too, No, the thing to do is to settle down and wait. If any of them get away, they'll make for the car."

With this, I quietly climbed into the tonneau, sat down on the floor of the car, and held my gun ready while I waited for developments.

They were not long in coming. That police captain was not taking chances nor wasting any finesse in his approach. With Sullivan at his elbow, he simply walked across the sand, for there was no front walk, to the house; the others had hurdled the low fence and vanished toward the back. O'Brien mounted the veranda, shoved open the front door, and walked inside. Sullivan followed him, leaving the door open and a square of light showing. For an instant nothing happened; then a police whistle shrilled out, and a revolver exploded sharply.

John Lee was at home, obviously.

Still, only silence followed. I craned over the side of the car, eagerly listening and watching. What was going on in that house, I could not tell. A low oath came to me, then O'Brien's voice raised sharply. An instant later, as I listened, I caught the hard "pad-pad" of feet on sand, and ducked down in the tonneau.

The car swayed as a man leaped to the running-board, fumbled with the front door, and slid in under the wheel. Without turning on his lights, he pressed the self-starter, and the engine thrummed into life. He shot in the gears and went sliding away. From the house behind came a startled shout, then a shot and another. One of those bullets passed through the top of the car above me. I kept quiet, a thrill of exultation passing through me as I realized the chance that had come. Undoubtedly the man behind the wheel was John Lee, and he would take me to Harpey if I only kept still!

A third shot from behind went wild. We took a corner on two wheels, presently passed the empty police car, and went roaring away toward the coast highway. The driver seemed to know his way, for he switched on his headlights only for an instant at a time. I could hear a low flood of curses pouring from him. Presently, as we neared the highway, he left his headlights on, and I crouched low lest he catch a reflection of my face in the windshield.

Reaching the highway, he turned toward San Francisco, moderated his speed to the legal thirty-five, and in a short time we were drawing in toward the city and getting past the cemeteries. By his driving, the man was in a hurry; he did not put on speed, but he went for the Twin Peaks road and took the curves like a maniac. At the top, I had a momentary glimpse of the city lights below, the Oakland and Alameda and Berkeley glitter—then we were going down the steep descent like an arrow. Presently we were past the park and heading straight downtown along Post Street.

His objective puzzled me, but I kept quiet, for it was evident that he was heading at some definite objective in the city, and I scarcely thought Harpey would be found in such a quarter. My uneasiness grew when, reaching Grant Street, he darted for Chinatown. I knew that once in that section he would have some chance of making a getaway, even under my gun, so I prepared to take him in hand. As I rose in the tonneau, he threw in the brakes and brought the car to a halt in front of a jewelry shop where the Chinatown tourists found many curios. As he did so, I put the gun against the back of his neck.

"Put 'em up and sit still!" I said.

He did so, but he was so startled and terrorized that he let out a wild yell, and a crowd began to gather instantly. Leaning over to get a good look at him in the street light, I was astounded to see that he was not John Lee at all. He was a perfect stranger, and quite a respectable looking one to boot. Just then, fortunately, two dicks of the Chinatown squad came shoving through the crowd; they knew me as a newspaper man, and I lost no time in appealing to them.

"Cap'n O'Brien wants this fellow at headquarters, and wants him quick," I said. "Pile in and have him drive us there, will you, boys? It's on the Brixton case."

"I hope you got a permit for that gun," growled one, as they piled in.

"It's in my pocket," I said. Then, when they got a good look at my prisoner, they whistled. One of them turned to me with a disturbed air.

"What's this, anyhow? This is Bradley—owns this jewelry store!"

"Get out of the crowd and talk later," I said.

They crowded in on Bradley, who was frightened and cowed, and did not demur at driving to headquarters. Thunderstruck as I was at finding him to be a well known merchant, I stuck to business, and we all marched up to the desk sergeant in company. Zimmerman was on hand, and joined us. I found that Sullivan and O'Brien had not yet returned.

"Now," I said to Bradley, "do you want to come across clean, or wait until the officers get in from Redwood Bluff?"

He made a slight, almost unconscious movement of his hand. One of the detectives seized him and explored his coat pocket, bringing into view a quantity of jewelry knotted in a handkerchief. There was a simultaneous cry.

"The Brixton sparklers!"

"I'll come clean!" exclaimed the jeweler in panic. "How'd I know what they were? A man had him drive me out there, kept me waiting a long while, and sold me these one by one. Said they were his wife's property, and she was dead."

"Let him tell it to O'Brien," I said to the sarge, and they took him away. I wanted to duck and get out of the publicity, but if Harpey was after me anyway, there was no use in hiding at this stage of the game. So I waited, staving off questions as well as I could.

It was only ten minutes later that O'Brien came along, bringing two Chinese prisoners and a limp, unconscious figure which was that of the chauffeur, Redtree—doped with chloral. Sullivan no sooner heard about me, and met my eye, than he let out a yell.

"It was you in the car—you got him!"

"Got somebody," I said, "but not Lee. Did he get away?"

"We never saw him," said Sullivan moodily. "We've got two Chinks, and a third put up a fight and passed out. He made a confession before he died. The chauffeur is in the clear."

"And Harpey?" I asked eagerly.

"Not implicated. Nobody knows him. Lee is the only one."

And Lee got clean away.

IV

IT WAS only nine o'clock when things were cleaned up enough for Sullivan and me to leave, with Zimmerman the sole reporter on the job, and everyone else warned the story would appear just as we wished to have it. Sullivan and I would pocket the reward, Captain O'Brien would assume the public credit, and everybody was happy all around. Redtree was completely exonerated. The only fly in the ointment was that we still had no line on Harpey.

Now, mark the time well. Sullivan was still hungry, so I called a taxi and we went down in style to Poodle Dog and had a French dinner. It was getting on toward ten o'clock when we paid the bill, lighted a good cigar, and stepped outside. The cobblestoned street was nearly deserted, and we walked to the curb before separating.

As we stood there, a taxi came down the hill and slowed. I had my hand raised to hail it, when something warned me—some sixth sense, or perhaps some movement which I scarcely realized seeing. My nerves were on edge, too. Crazy as appeared the impulse, I did not resist it, but dropped to the pavement and kicked Sullivan's legs out from beneath him as I dropped.

At that very instant, the taxi erupted flame and bullets—two guns going at short range. They missed us clean. I rolled across the sidewalk, and heard another bullet strike within an inch of my head. Then the taxi roared and was gone, plunging down to the corner and around on two wheels. It had vanished before I got on my feet.

"Beat it," said Sullivan, and we darted to the corner. Pursuit was hopeless. We looked back at the inquiring crowd, then at each other. Sullivan grinned.

"That's the way they bumped off Jerry," he observed. "Harpey's got his eye on us, eh?"

"He's a fast worker," I agreed. "I can't go back to Friedman's now."

"Let's you and me, sir-r," said Sullivan thoughtfully, "go hunt us a new home."

We did it.

IV

POPPY GOLD

*Harpey, That Master Mind Among Criminals,
Here Takes a Hand at a Different Game—
and Almost Succeeds at It. Weird Enterprises
Originate in San Francisco's Chinatown*

I

FOR TWO days now, Terry Sullivan and I had been in hiding at a small hotel between Market Street and Chinatown, in the very center of downtown San Francisco. The big detective piloted me there, and there we stayed close. The patronage at this hotel consisted chiefly of government men and upstate politicians; you might see anyone there from Jack Considine to his honor the mayor, and it was the safest place in town for us. By the second night of our stay, however, we were both tired of the confinement. It was a nice fix for the best headquarters detective in the city and Dick Clews, soldier of fortune and ex-officer in the Chinese army!

"If we don't hear something soon, sir-r," said Sullivan, as we smoked together in my room after dinner, that second night, "I'll be takin' a chance or two."

"You can't," I said. "Not only for our own sake, but for that of Lew Friedman. He's a cripple and helpless. If that devil Harpey once learned that he was behind us in this fight, Harpey would wipe him out inside of an hour. You know how clever that scoundrel is."

Sullivan bit at his pipe and scowled. "Him and his lieutenant, John Lee. They know we're after 'em, sir-r, but Lee's the one to be lookin' out for. He has a life sentence for murder hangin' over him if we catch him, and a reward of two thousand on his head, glory be!"

"You're wrong there," I said, with truth. "Harpey's the head and brains of the gang, and Lee only executes his orders. Friedman knows where we are and can reach us. Headquarters knows, and so does the Oakland detective bureau. If any of them get a line on Harpey, they'll inform us."

"But Harpey's niece don't know," said Sullivan gloomily.

That was checkmate, sure enough. Claire Maynard, who called herself Harpey's niece and who was somehow forced or terrorized into aiding him, had supplied me with clues to his activities, thus enabling us to fight him; but we had completely failed either to run down Harpey or to get his murderous Chinese lieutenant. And now Claire Maynard had no earthly idea where to reach me. She knew nothing about Lew Friedman, who was the only man able to decipher the peculiar code used between Harpey and his lieutenant.

"We've done well so far," I ruminated aloud. "We know that Harpey stays out of the game, sends word to Lee, and the latter pulls the job; and we've made a pile of money from the rewards we've collected. None of Harpey's gang knows about him—they all think Lee is the big boss."

"Even if Miss Maynard could he reachin' us," added Sullivan, "what could we do? Your friend Friedman would have to translate the stuff, and we can't go near him."

"Don't you think it," I said warmly. "Lew Friedman may be a cripple, but he's in this fight to beat Harpey—and he's a fighter! When it comes to brains, Lew has them. He knows the

Chinese language inside out, and he knows Harpey. If we did get a clue, I'd go see Friedman."

"And take a chance on Harpey's gettin' wise to the game, sir-r?"

"You bet. We'd have to depend on Friedman, anyway—"

The telephone on the corner table tinkled, and we both jumped. We had a case of nerves. And no wonder, since Harpey's gunmen had come within an ace of riddling us both from a taxicab.

"Hello?" I said, reaching the instrument.

A rumbling voice responded. "Headquarters speaking, sir. Anybody there named Terry Sullivan?"

I handed the telephone to the detective. He listened a moment, then looked over at me.

"Cap'n O'Brien speaking, sir-r. He says there's a letter for you at headquarters. Do you want it sent over?"

"A letter? Then it's from Miss Maynard—yes! Can you get him to send a headquarters car with it? We can't trust a taxi, and I'll have to go to Friedman with the letter—"

Terry Sullivan could get anything he wanted from head-quarters, and set down the telephone with a grin of delight. He ranked as detective sergeant himself.

"On the way, Mr. Clews! Both of us going, I s'pose?"

"Yes, sure! Give me that phone, will you?"

I called Lew Friedman's number. Lew, thanks to an old spinal injury, was an almost hopeless cripple; he could sit up only a few hours a day, though of late he had evinced some improvement, due perhaps to the mental stimulus of our fight against Harpey. By good luck I found him up, and the nurse said we could come out for an hour—that nurse was none too glad to hear from me, either. She claimed that I had a bad effect on her patient, which was true.

In six minutes we were down in the hotel lobby, hats pulled down and faces wrapped in mufflers. When the headquarters car came to the curb outside, we stepped out and got in very quickly, and the chauffeur started off at once. He knew his business.

"Run out Post Street," I told him, and gave him Friedman's number in Millard Street, one of the smaller thoroughfares in the hilly section of the city. He passed the letter to me, and I pocketed it with a sigh at the impossibility of examining it at once.

"How d'you know it's from her, sir-r?" growled Sullivan curiously, and I laughed.

"Have faith, you big mick!"

He grunted. "If she can tip us off to Harpey's jobs, why not to the old divil himself?"

"She's afraid, for some reason; thinks he'd wipe us out. If I could only get a chance to talk with her—well, let it go. Here's Millard Street."

We roared up the hill and stopped, told the chauffeur to wait, and entered the house. The nurse received us and passed us into the library.

Lew Friedman looked distinctly improved during the past two days. His bright blue eyes were snapping with energy, his mane of white hair was touseled, and the books strewn around his work-table showed that he had been studying. When he had greeted us, he leaned back in his wheelchair and snapped a word at me.

"Well?"

Oddly enough, I had not the least doubt as to the source of that letter. When I produced it, all three of us stared down at it, and a thrill ran over me at sight of the girl's handwriting. Someone pointed to the postmark.

"Mailed this mornin' at the Post Street office!" he exclaimed. Friedman nodded, and as there was nothing further to be learned from the envelope, ripped it open. A single sheet of paper fell out, upon which he seized avidly. A single Chinese character met our eyes:

Beneath this was written, in pencil, *Sent J. M. Nealy, 107 Tampon St., Oakland.* Nothing else. Friedman studied it a moment, then relaxed and shook his head, as he looked up.

"Miss Maynard wrote that," he said. "She copied it rather poorly. We've already conjectured that she acts as Harpey's secretary or assistant; somehow, he has her in his power and can make use of her. She may have to act as go-between from him to Lee. He keeps himself well under cover, you see."

"But what's it mean, sir-r?" demanded Sullivan eagerly. Friedman smiled.

"It means that I'll have to work," he said. "There are several characters almost identical, and this might be any one of them, but each comes from a different ancient character. Hand me down the Gloss, will you, Dick? There's only one thing certain—that devil Lee is at the Oakland address given. He's the only person who could comprehend Harpey's ciphers, for none but a well educated Chinaman could understand it. If you want to nab Lee, you'd better get over to Oakland tonight. Now the writing stand, Dick—thanks."

I gave him the brass writing stand, with water and brushes and Chinese ink, and he fell to work over his books. Sullivan, meantime, seated himself at the telephone and called the Oakland headquarters, with whom he engaged in conversation. I watched Lew Friedman, who was laboring away in tense concentration, running down ancient characters in his Chinese volumes. Presently a sharp exclamation broke from him. He brushed a character, then leaned back and drew a long breath.

"Got it, I think! What did you find out from Oakland, Sullivan?"

The detective was quivering with suppressed eagerness.

"We'll go over in the car, sir-r. The Oakland chief himself will be waiting in another car with a squad. They'll follow us. This address is out in the sticks somewheres at the end o' town,

toward the valley boulevard. That headquarters chauffeur of
ours is from Oakland and a good bye he is; he'll know where
to be findin' the place. Glory be, we got that divil Lee this time!
What's the message mean, sir?"

Friedman smiled thoughtfully. "I'm not so certain just what
it means, to tell the honest truth; it's largely guesswork to me.
I take it to mean, however, that Harpey is sending something
to Lee. This man Harpey is mixed up in all sorts of things, as
we know. Over in China he was largely responsible for the
opium revival—he was agent for the Macao factories and did
a lot of harm before he was kicked out. I suppose you've both
often seen these Chinamen around town carrying a long porter's bar on their shoulders with a load?"

We nodded, for it was a familiar sight in San Francisco and
the bay cities, where the yellow folk cling to their own ways.
On almost any ferryboat may be seen a Chinese porter, carrying across his shoulders a long pole or bar with the load balanced
at either end. Lew picked up his brush and illustrated his translation of the character.

"This is the ancient character *jenn*, which
may mean either a weight or to endure, to bear,
and so forth. Here's the representation of a
porter's pole, with a line at either end to represent the load; and across the center is drawn a
third line, but much longer, to represent the man who is carrying it.

"Now," he went on thoughtfully, "we know already that, to
any chance eye this character would show only its modern
meaning of a weight, and would betray nothing. But to Lee, I
think, it would mean that Harpey was sending him something,
carried by porters in this fashion. Just what is being sent, we
don't know."

"And we don't care a hoot neither," broke in Sullivan excit-
edly. "The big thing is to nab Lee, and we just about got time
to make the seven-fifty auto ferry!"

"All right." Friedman smiled a little wistfully as we seized our coats. "I sure wish I could go along with you fellows, but I'll have to make the best of things as they are. Now, don't be too sure of your luck, Dick! Remember, that girl posted her letter to you this morning; the chances are that the original message went to Lee last night or yesterday. Since Harpey is on the trail of you two men, he may somehow suspect that the girl is tipping off his hand; this thing may be a fake. Still, notice the alias of Nealy! A word that Chinese could pronounce, and one that embodies Lee's name. Well, go ahead and good luck to you."

We left, and it was a nervous ride down to the ferry, and across the bay to Oakland. Any person in the crowds around us might be a potential assassin, for it was certain that Harpey was combing the bay district for me and Sullivan. He had every thug in the Mission at his command—and once we were recognized, the bullets would come swiftly!

I I

LEAVING THE ferry, we drove slowly through Oakland toward the valley highway, and Sullivan declared that the local police car had picked us up and was following, but I took little interest. To tell the truth, this looked to me like nothing but an opportunity to get Lee, and all my concern was with Claire Maynard.

The girl's face lingered heavily with me—a delicate oval contour, crowned with gold, eyes like blue stars; yet she was no silly fool to be easily coerced by Harpey. Probably she thought the man her uncle, but I refused to believe it. Had she been some weak creature who was merely being used as a tool, I would still have been only too glad to help her; as it was, she was a girl of character and personality, and there hung the mystery. I must admit that my feeling toward her was deeper than any surface chivalry. She was a girl in a thousand.

The evening was still young when we approached the neighborhood of Tampon Street. It was on the outskirts of town; a district of scattered bungalows of the poorer sort, nearly all of them having a vanguard of poultry houses. From here to Petaluma, chickens and eggs formed the standard side-line of every small householder.

"There's your street," and the chauffeur nodded to a sparsely built-up street as we passed by. "Leave the cars along here, eh?"

Sullivan assented, and in a moment we drew up. When we alighted, the second car halted behind us and switched off the lights. The Oakland chief and his squad, all in plain clothes, joined us, and animated conversation ensued.

It was settled that Sullivan and I should have the dubious honor of making a frontal assault, with our own chauffeur to aid us, while the Oakland squad spread out around and behind the place to await any alarm from us. The whole endeavor was to make sure of getting Lee. Just as this was arranged, Sullivan gave a sharp exclamation and pointed to the corner of the street.

There, passing beneath the arc light and sharply defined, was the figure of a Chinaman, a long pole across his shoulders weighted down at either end by bundles of wicker chairs. He shuffled along, slightly stooped, with that plodding, patient tread of his kind.

"Grab him and do it now," said Sullivan, without bothering to explain to the Oakland men, "but don't let him squawk."

Two of them slipped away. The Chinaman was obviously suspicious, for under the light he paused and looked at the two men hurrying toward him, then he drooped and went on. A word from them checked him. He made some response, then began to lift his voice shrilly as though in anger. One of them checked that game at the outset with a heavy hand. They gagged the poor devil and marched him back to the cars. He was ironed in one of them, while the squad went to work on his load of chairs.

They know what to look for and how to seek it in San Francisco. In two minutes Sullivan had one of the chairs apart and showed a bamboo leg heavy with a dark, congealed substance.

"Dope," he said succinctly. "That blows Lee's game. Come on, sir-r."

Our chauffeur joined us, and we walked to Tampon Street, then turned down it to seek our objective. There were but half a dozen houses on either side of the block; it was impossible to see their numbers because of the obscurity here, and any close approach might give warning of our business. The third house on the right showed light around the window-edges, and a dark automobile was standing in the street before it. Sullivan pointed.

"Harpey uses cars in his business, so let's—"

"I'll do it," I said quickly, remembering how I had met Claire Maynard driving Harpey's car with a false license plate, a few days previously. "She may be here, Sullivan."

"G'wan, then," he growled reluctantly. "We got to give the other byes time to spread out anyhow."

I walked on toward where the car stood. Once more we had proven the exactness of Lew Friedman's work, the precision with which he translated that singular cipher system used by Harpey; and it was perfectly obvious that among his other activities Harpey was distributing opium via his lieutenant Lee. Probably he smuggled it into San Francisco, and then sent it out to the bay cities.

This mattered little to me, however, for my thoughts were upon Claire Maynard. Nearing the car, I recognized it as one of the same make as that which the girl had been driving when I encountered her in San Francisco—possibly it was the same car! The license plates would tell. Could she be here, then? My pulses thrilled to the thought, both with hope and with fear, for she must not be caught in this opium raid.

The car was an open model, and as I approached it with sharp scrutiny I was convinced that it was empty. Once beside it, I verified this fact, then went to the rear and felt the license plates with exploring fingers. The raised figures told me what I wanted to know. It was Harpey's car.

I straightened up and gazed reflectively at the house, which stood thirty feet back from the street, with a fence on either side but none in front. So far as Miss Maynard was concerned, I could count absolutely on Terry Sullivan. He alone knew the whole inside story of our fight, and would go to any length to protect the girl who was our only link with Harpey. And yet it was impossible to restrain these men on the bare chance that—

The front door of the house flew open, and in the lighted doorway appeared the figure of Claire Maynard. She was bare-headed, but wearing a long driving ulster, and swinging in her hand was a motoring helmet.

Then, as she stepped outside, the door went half-shut again, but I saw that a man had followed her out and was detaining her. His voice reached me clearly.

"Wait!" he exclaimed, none too gently. "I tell you it can't be long till the last man comes in, and—"

"I've waited too long now, thank you," said the girl's clear, resolute voice, ringing against the night like a silver bell. It held a distinct note of contempt, of anger. "I'll not spend another minute in this house—if I wait anywhere, it'll be in the car."

"You hold on, young lady," responded the man. "I got to call Lee before you go. You ain't goin' till he gives the word, and that's flat."

"Don't you dare touch me, you hophead!" snapped the girl in anger, and I realized that both of them were moving toward the car. "Call him if you want to. I'll wait here in the car. The payment for the last batch can wait until next week, anyway. You dare lay a finger on me, and my uncle will make you suffer!"

"I don't know your blamed uncle and don't give a darn," growled the man. "You come on back here, or I'll learn you something! Think you're too fine for me, do you? No skirt is going to pull that stuff on me—"

The figures plunged forward dimly; I sensed that the girl was trying to reach the car while the man was leaping to detain her, clutching at her. He reached her, too, caught her long coat in so fierce a grip that the fabric ripped—and just then I reached him, with a hundred and eighty pounds of Dick Clews behind the smash.

He went down as though shot, and I afterward learned that his jaw was smashed. A dark, heavy object fell to the ground as the girl pulled clear. I swooped on it and crammed it into my side pocket. Claire Maynard had darted into the car, and in two words I told the alarmed and frightened girl who I was. She had already started the engine. Two men went pounding past me toward the house.

"Get 'em, Sullivan!" I called, to let the detective know I was all right, and then leaped to the running-board of the car. Claire Maynard was just throwing in the clutch.

"Easy, now," I said quietly. "You'll not be bothered in this business, Miss Maynard. Lee is the one they're after—"

"You—Dick Clews!" she cried softly, frantically. "Oh—but they can't get Lee, they can never get him! Hang on; stoop down while I get you away—quickly! There are two men in the house across the street—they'll take you and your friends from behind! I didn't know they were there before—hang on, now, hang on."

With this excited, chattering speech she had the car in motion. She was ignorant of our strength, naturally, and thought there were only two or three of us. Yet for an instant I did not get the sense of her agonized and rapid utterance.

Then, glancing back at the figures of Sullivan and the police chauffeur outlined in the bungalow doorway, I saw one of them pitch sideways, and from across the street came a rifle crack. A second followed it, and the bullet actually went through my hat.

Infernally clever Harpey, who took no chances! Here he had two men posted in the house across the street from that of

Lee—two guards, evidently, with rifles to use and the will to use them. Another shot cracked out. *"Ping-g!"* The bullet smashed through the hood and instantly the engine began to limp.

"Stop!" I cried desperately, from my place on the running-board beside her. "There's no danger—I have more men."

"You don't know!" she flung at me. "I'll take you away from them—I must get back to San José at once."

She had the car around the corner on two wheels, then brought it to a sharp stop an instant later. From behind us were coming shouts, shots, the shrill scream of police whistles. Before I knew what she was up to, Claire Maynard had leaped out, flung up the hood, and was looking at the engine.

"A spark plug smashed—give me another from the door pocket under your hand!" she snapped. "Pliers, too—"

I fumbled in the door pocket, got the pliers and an extra plug, and joined her. She snatched them from me and leaned over the engine, working.

"So you live in San José?" I demanded. "Harpey is there, then? Tell me where, quickly! You're safe from him—I have friends more powerful than he."

She did not look up, but spoke hurriedly, and yet with a certain dread composure, as though the pressure of her fate could not be withstood.

"Oh, I wish I could, Mr. Clews! But you don't know. If I don't return tonight he'll tell everything. He knows what will put my father in jail—nothing really wrong, just a technical crime—but the law won't spare him. And you don't know my uncle. He's terrible, and he has implicated me in things—"

I caught her arm, and drew her up so that under the street light her eyes met mine.

"Miss Maynard, I guarantee to protect you from Harpey, and your father, too," I said earnestly. "There's another man with me in this fight—an older man. He and I are working together. He knew Harpey in China. Now tell me, quickly! All I want is the address. You need not go back to him—"

"You mean it!" For an instant her eyes widened on mine, and in them I read everything I had not dared hope to see. "Yes— you are not afraid—perhaps it is possible after all! I thought there was no hope—"

"There's every hope," I broke in curtly. "Where's Harpey?"

"The yellow house—"

A sharp cry checked her speech, bursting from her like a wail of agony. A dark shape sprang out of the darkness, a pistol roared, and again I felt the shock of a bullet striking, and was knocked backward by it. Then, as I fell, there came the pound of running feet, and the sharp, deadly voice of Lee broke into my dimming senses.

"Got that devil anyhow—in with you! Pile in there."

Everything went black.

I I I

WHEN I woke up, Terry Sullivan and one of the Oakland men were working over me. I got on my feet and stared at them dazedly. Seeing that I was all right, the Oakland man ran to rejoin his chief and companions, who were approaching. Sullivan held me upright.

"Divil a trace o' blood, sir-r—"

"Lee got me—here in the side," I gasped, and turned to the street light, with a stab of pain. Yet there was no blood. My exploring fingers brought forth a heavy object from my coat pocket—the same which I had picked up after freeing Claire Maynard from her assailant. It was a bag of money, gold by feel, and one side was badly ripped.

"Glory be!" said Sullivan in an awed voice. He leaned forward and probed the little sack, then produced an irregular object. "The bullet! But where did this money come from?"

"Miss Maynard dropped it," I said, and suddenly comprehended everything. "Harpey sent her here to get the money for the opium from Lee—and Sullivan! She was on the point of telling me everything when Lee showed up and two other men. Thought they killed me—sure I'm not hit?"

"Divil a bit," said Sullivan. "Black and blue, knocked out for a bit—but not hit. There's the bullet from the money sack, sir-r. And will ye keep quiet about the money, now? All yellow byes, by the looks, and what's the use to be handing it over?"

He shoved the little sack into his pocket. I hardly realized his action, for I was thinking of my own miraculous escape. Only that bag of gold coin had saved me from Lee's bullet.

As for Lee himself, the other two men, and Claire Maynard—I had to make swift decision, for the Oakland squad were upon us. Only the girl knew that I was aware of their destination, of the city forty miles away where Harpey kept under cover. It was a temptation to set the wires and radio at work to find the car and the fugitives, but Lee was not to be caught that way. He would abandon that car within five miles, and reach San José in some other fashion. Meantime, I had the clue, knew where to work.

"Missed the big bird!" said the Oakland chief. "Got two white men and six Chinks and a big haul of dope—but no Lee. I've left a man there and the wagon's on the way. What's this about you bein' shot, Clews?"

"Lee got away in a car, thought he'd killed me," I said, laughing to find myself well and sound instead of dead. "I've got the car's number—"

I gave it to him, and with his men he broke for his car to reach headquarters and send out the alarm. An excited crowd was gathering fast, so Sullivan and I made haste to our own car—but alone. Our chauffeur was back there in the house with the prisoners, shot through the body, but not mortally hurt. As we got our car started, the clangor of gongs bespoke the arriving ambulance and patrol wagon.

"Where are you heading for?" I demanded, as Sullivan took the wheel and we started.

"Oakland headquarters," he said. "We got to get this cleaned up. It's a cinch they won't find Lee's car, sir-r. Ain't it the divil how he does be slippin' out of our hands? And what about the girl?"

"She went with them," I said, and suppressed a bitter oath. "Lee cheated me again in the very moment of victory, Sullivan. Still, I know where Harpey is located. He's in San José, in a yellow house. Lee's bullet cut the rest short. Don't forget to let the Oakland squad have all the credit for this job, now! And cut it short, for I want to get in touch with Friedman at once, and you'll have to make report to your own headquarters."

Sullivan swore under his breath, for he was wild with fury at Lee having escaped us. He did not speak again until we reached headquarters. Then, as he climbed out of the car and I said that I would wait for him, he thrust the little bag of gold at me.

"Take care o' this, sir-r."

As I sat there in the car, waiting for him to return, I played with the gold pieces; through the bullet-rent bag, my fingers found the coins bent and misshapen from their contact with the bullet. Presently Sullivan returned.

"All clear, sir-r," he said, and climbed in.

"What are you going to do with this money?" I asked.

"Well, sir-r, it's up to you," he returned, hesitant. "It was in me mind that if we got Miss Maynard away, it would be givin' her a stake to start wid, praise be! I dunno about the rights of it—"

"Neither do I, and care less," I said, and stowed the bag in my pocket again. "We'll keep it for her, Sullivan—good idea! How did Lee get out of the house?"

Sullivan swore fluently. "He was never in it, sir-r. The slick divil was in the house acrost the street! And now he's gone—"

"And the stage shifts to San José," I said. "Now let's go home."

So we went.

V

DEATH AND THE WOMAN

On One Side a Young Newspaper Man—
On the Other the Forces of the Underworld
Rallying to the Support of an Acknowledged
Leader. And the Result a Prize Beyond Price.
No Wonder Such an Epic Fight Was Staged

THE TRAINED nurse adjusted Lew Friedman in his wheelchair and then, at his command, left us alone. She gave me a warning look in departing, for, due to an old spinal injury, Friedman could only sit up a small part of the day and was forbidden any excitement—but she did not know of the grim fight that we were carrying on. Only one other person in San Francisco knew of it.

Lew relaxed in his chair and smiled at me, rumpling up his thick white hair. The keen flash in his blue eye belied the smile, however.

"Where's Sergeant Sullivan?" he asked, naming the one other man who was in our confidence.

"At headquarters, arranging to get authority in San José. We're going there today."

Friedman nodded. "If only I weren't tied to this chair! Well, I can't give you much help, I'm afraid, but you've learned definite news at last. First, Harpey has his headquarters in San José; second, you've driven that devil Lee to take refuge with his chief. Harpey knows you and Sullivan are after him, but he doesn't suspect my share in the game—"

"Hold on," I said earnestly. "Lew, I'm horribly afraid that Claire Maynard is in danger. In my brief talk with her last night, I discovered that she really believes herself to be Harpey's niece, and thinks that unless she obeys Harpey he'll send her father to jail. For her father's sake, she stays with Harpey, who has used her as a go-between in reaching that rascal, Lee. Last night she was ready to come with me and leave Harpey, trusting that we'd be able to arrange everything—then Lee showed up, knocked me out, and vanished with her. He may have guessed that she has been tipping us off to Harpey's plans. If so, heaven help her!"

Friedman's lips tightened. "Harpey's a man of tremendous ability gone to the bad," he affirmed. "As a brainy criminal, he has no equal today. Lee is an escaped murderer with a big reward on him dead or alive—a deadly snake. We need to fear Harpey's brains and Lee's action. Lee, an American-born Chinese, is horribly dangerous. He thinks that you're dead, and the next move will be to get Sullivan. Fortunately, my activity is not suspected."

"Fortunately for you," I added. Indeed, poor Friedman would have little chance were it known that his keen brain lay behind our fight on Harpey. "But what about the girl—Claire Maynard? She's the one who's in danger, unless I'm much mistaken."

"Not in immediate danger," amended Friedman thoughtfully. "Harpey would not scruple to murder her in a minute, but we may assume that he still needs her. Harpey stays in the background and hides behind his agents. If he thinks that she has betrayed him, then of course he would not hesitate to wipe her out—but he would do it in a way that would be useful to him. You can't estimate Harpey's brains too highly, Dick."

The nurse entered and spoke to me. "Mr. Clews, your friend Mr. Sullivan is here to—"

Sullivan calmly brushed the nurse aside, ignored her disdainful air, and came puffing into the room. The big detective, who was the only other person in full cognizance of our fight on Harpey, and who was my assistant iin the actual work, nodded to us and dropped into a chair.

"This here street is the steepest dommed hill in San Francisco," he panted. "Glory be, the headquarters car had a blowout and I run the rest of the way."

"In a hurry?" inquired Friedman, laughing, yet with an alert look.

"Aye, sir-r!" Sullivan, who was in plain clothes as usual, put a hand into his pocket. "I got the use of a headquarters car and chauffeur, and we've fixed things with San José so we'll get all the help we want. Then this thing blew in by mail, a minute before I left, and I came along in a blessed hurry."

He threw an envelope into Friedman's lap and sat back, grimly expectant. I leaned over the chair and looked, with a sudden thrill—but disappointment seized me. The writing was not in the neat hand of Claire Maynard; it was in a blunt, angular script, and the envelope was addressed to me or to Sullivan, in care of police headquarters. And suddenly, perhaps because of my recent conversation with Lew Friedman, a subtle sense of danger, of impending fury, came into my mind.

The postmark proved that this letter had been posted, early this same morning, at San José.

Friedman tore open the envelope, his thin features set in tense lines, and drew forth a small oblong of paper—peculiar paper—upon which was brushed a single Chinese character, which meant less than nothing to my eyes.

At the same time, even I could tell that Claire Maynard had never copied this character, which was fairly intricate. Only a skilled calligraphist or painter can limn the writing of the celestials with any success. This single character was brushed as delicately as though set down by the hand of an etcher.

Friedman let the paper fall into his lap, with a gesture that expressed finality, futility, hopelessness. He looked up, met Sullivan's intent gaze, and his thinly ascetic features were bleak and stony.

"I'm sorry to say, sergeant, that it's your move—Harpey's after you now," he said quietly. "This was addressed either to Clews or to you, showing that Lee reported Dick to be dead— and except for a very lucky accident, Dick would be dead, indeed. Harpey brushed this himself; the paper is his own fine imported rice-paper, the ink his own expensive ink of the highest quality. Finally, we believe that Lee escaped to San José, so that he and Harpey are now together, and Harpey would not be sending the cipher to anyone else. Harpey evidently believes that you have in some way stumbled on to the meaning of his secret writing. This is a trap."

Sullivan leaned forward and growled, his square-jawed face hardest.

"A trap, sir-r? But traps use bait."

"Right." Friedman tapped the paper in his lap. "The bait to this trap is Claire Maynard."

"Explain it, for heaven's sake!" I burst out impatiently. "Your argument may be conceded, Lew—but what's the meaning of it all? What does this character imply? If Harpey has set a trap, why didn't he make Claire Maynard write this thing?"

"Why should he think that Sullivan or even you could detect such differences in the calligraphy in this paper, in the ink? He knows you're not experts. He doesn't dream that I am in the game—for he knows of me, or did know of me in the past."

"Do you want your books and work-table to look up this character?" I demanded.

Friedman smiled thinly. "No, Dick, not this time. Hand me a sheet of paper and the inkstand and I'll show you in a moment what it means—it's a well known character which today means fear, dignity, or majesty. But this *wei* meant something else again in the ancient and original form of the character, and as a matter of fact it has been only slightly changed by the scribes. It's really an ideograph, an idea presented in picture form—"

I put the reading table across Friedman's wheelchair, handed him some paper, and got down the brass stand with its Chinese writing equipment. Lew took a brush, and when it was inked he swiftly drew two characters which were as exquisitely perfect as the work of Harpey, or more so.

"Here, first," he explained, "is the picture of a barbed halberd with a crescent head, and the straight line inside it stands for a wound. I'm not saying it's a good picture; but the ancient Chinese weapons were unwieldy and wonderful things, and there it is. The meaning of this character *su* is death, from the combination of weapon and wound.

"This second figure is merely the picture of a girl, lacking the head, standing in the ritual attitude of a Chinese girl; it represents a woman. Now, place this inside the first character, and what's the answer? Simply, the fear which the thought of death brings to a woman, or supposedly so. Across the thousands of years, it has come to mean dignity or majesty. But we know that Harpey's cipher refers to the ancient derivation of the characters used. Therefore it's easy to conjecture that this represents a threat of death to Claire Maynard—he wants you to think she's in danger of death. Understand? He has baited his trap with the girl."

Friedman paused. Sullivan was scowling blackly, but remained silent. I leaned forward and picked up the message from Harpey, simply to compare the beauty of his writing with that of my friend. Now that I had in mind the origin and explanation of these hen-tracks, it was easy to see that the countless generations of scribes had not changed them greatly, though they had been abbreviated for more rapid writing.

"It might mean another thing," I said. "It might mean that Harpey had ordered Lee to kill Miss Maynard, and that she had managed to get the message sent to us—"

Friedman smiled sardonically. "Exactly what Harpey wants you to think."

"But where's the house?" demanded Sullivan heavily. "All we know is that Harpey's in San José, and that's the biggest town in the Santa Clara valley."

By chance I laid down the paper wrong side up, and Friedman seized upon it avidly.

"Ah! What's this?"

Penciled on the back of the paper was an address, and the first glance told me that it was in the writing of Claire Maynard. The address was 3105 Claridon Street.

"She wrote it," I explained, as the three of us crowded in to look. Friedman nodded.

"Yes, probably under compulsion. If she had herself been able to write you, she'd have used plain English. You can depend on it, this is not Harpey's address. If you go there, you'll be playing his game."

I stood up. "I've knocked about the world a few years, Lew, and sometimes it's necessary to play the other fellow's game to—"

"Don't be a fool!" he interjected sharply. "You haven't the brains to cope with Harpey."

"Maybe not, but I'm damned stubborn at times, and this is one of the times, Lew. That girl is in trouble, and I'm going."

"Then," said the big detective, heaving himself up out of his chair, "let's go, sir-r!"

II

IT IS only a forty-mile boulevard run to San José, and in the fleet police car we covered it in an hour and a half. As we passed the great Jesuit college in Santa Clara and crossed the invisible boundary into the city of San José, Sullivan turned to me perplexedly.

"Shall I tell the chauffeur to make for headquarters first, sir-r?" he asked. "They'll give us all the help we want."

"If this is really a trap for you," I returned, "Harpey or his gang will be watching for that very thing; they may even have police headquarters under observation, waiting for you to show up there. Besides, every time we've dragged your police friends into this affair, we've lost out. Suppose we go slow and look the ground over, first."

"We'll do that same, praise be," said Sullivan, and instructed the police chauffeur.

We had no fear of being seen and recognized, for we had lowered the rain-curtains of the car and could see without being observed. San José, beautiful as it was with its broad avenues and great trees, its splendid public buildings and handsome private dwellings, registered little impression on me as we drove across town, for my thoughts were with Claire Maynard and her position, not to mention our own. We had no idea what to expect. One thing that, in our hurry, we had not taken into account was Harpey's position. He and his Chinese lieutenant Lee must be next door, and desperate in the endeavor to get rid of me and Sullivan, for we had baulked them repeatedly, had practically destroyed their criminal organization, and about half the population of northern California was on the lookout for a glimpse of Lee's face and the reward. Of Harpey himself we had not so much a photograph, and I was the only one who knew what his general appearance was like. Now, fortunately, Harpey thought me dead, or at least out of the fight.

Again, that little taunt of Friedman's, true though it undoubtedly was, rankled in me. My brains were no match for those of Harpey, yet I had no hesitation in pitting myself against him; he might outwit me, yet I was resolved to fight and beat him.

"Here's your street, Sarge!" came the voice of the chauffeur from in front. "Looks like the next block is yours."

He slowed down. We were in a well-built street of bungalows and undistinguished residences. Ahead of us on the left was an unpretentious hotel occupying the corner—a square brick building with shops below. Diagonally opposite the hotel was a large frame house, the first in the block. I tapped the driver's shoulder.

"Stop in front of that hotel."

"What for?" demanded Sullivan, and jerked his thumb. "That's our house, that gray frame on the corner yonder, first one in the block. 3105 is the number, and I'll gamble it's that same house—"

"There's nothing to mark this as a police car except the license plates," I said, "and we'll gamble on that much. Harpey or Lee has a man on watch, you may be sure. If that's our house, what do we want to do? Keep our eyes open and on it. If we stop at that hotel we can get a room that'll overlook the diagonally opposite corner, and we'll have two sides of the place in view. Also, the car will prevent our being seen as we get into the hotel."

"Praise be, sir-r, it's a fine head ye have!" exclaimed Sullivan admiringly.

It was not yet quite noon, and we had the day ahead of us. The chauffeur drew up ahead of the hotel entrance, which was a stairway ascending to the second floor, and I gave him his instructions.

"Go get two pairs of prismatics—rent or buy them—and lay the car up in a garage somewhere near here. Get some lunch for us all, as we can't leave here until after dark. Then come back and get a room. I'll have one saved for you."

He saluted. Sullivan had spread the fact that I had been a captain in the Chinese army, and it helped me greatly where the police were concerned. The detective and I slipped into the hotel entrance, our figures covered by the car, and tramped upstairs to the second floor, where the office was located, in what I imagine to be the purely California second-rate hotel style.

We rang a bell, the landlady appeared, and in ten minutes we were comfortably ensconced in the corner room on the second floor, with that adjoining reserved for the chauffeur. We had two windows, and an uninterrupted view of the corner house diagonally opposite us. Sullivan studied, the house from behind the curtain, then settled our only doubt.

"That's the house—I can see the number, praise be!" he declared, and rose. "Say the word, sir-r, and I'll be callin' the wagon and do the job right now!"

I shook my head. "No. The main thing with me, Sullivan, is Miss Maynard. There's little doubt that Harpey has discovered how she has been tipping us off, and some scheme has been framed up to murder her and kill you at the same time—if you come. Lee will do the job. What we must do, is to get her away in safety."

We settled down to wait. In half an hour the chauffeur rejoined us, bringing the provisions and binoculars. We ate in our room, as there was no dining-room in the hotel, and no way of reaching the restaurant below without leaving the hotel entrance. Then we drew up chairs and set ourselves to keep watch on the house.

We had a difficult problem to solve before we could attempt anything. Here was a trap which had been set for Sullivan; presumably Miss Maynard was inside the house, too. Lee was certain to be in charge of the job. Now, Lee must have expected Sullivan to surround the house with police and raid him, sometime during the coming night; how, then, did Lee purpose to make his escape? If we were to spring the trap and baulk Lee, we must learn this first. Nor did I discount the possibility that Claire Maynard might be already dead.

The house was a gray bungalow with airplane upper story. It lacked a garage, and its curtained windows showed no signs of life within. It stood on a crowded, narrow lot and looked absolutely innocuous; that such an eminently respectable dwelling could be a death-trap, was hard to credit, especially in view of its quietness. Harpey had had only a few hours in which to formulate his plans, get off the cipher message to me or Sullivan, and get ready; yet there was nothing about the house to indicate anything out of the ordinary. Indeed, two painters were at work, in the leisurely California style, retarring the roofs.

"Harpey wouldn't be havin' painters there unless he wanted 'em," observed Sullivan.

This was true, and I probed for the reason vainly. Time passed, and brought nothing. Then, at two-thirty, a Chinaman came shuffling up the side street and turned in at the back door of the house. He did not reappear. I had just opened my mouth to comment on this, when the front house-door opened—and out came Harpey himself.

For an instant I could not believe my eyes. There he was, as I had once before seen him—a great, almost gigantic figure of a man with grayish beard, and well dressed. He carried a stick, which is not so usual in California cities as in New York, and looked the peak of prosperity. I turned to the chauffeur, who was reading a newspaper behind us.

"Wake up, there! Get out and follow that man—and grab him if you can do it quietly! That's Harpey himself, the head of the gang. Or wait—don't grab him! Follow him wherever he goes. We want to find out where he's located. Follow him and report to us here by phone."

The chauffeur caught up his hat and vanished hurriedly. Sullivan swore in excitement.

"So that's Harpey, is it? Then—look there, sir-r! It's herself!"

Harpey stood at the bunaglow steps, and in the doorway behind him I saw the figure of Claire Maynard. The prismatics brought her face close to me; a face pallid with fright, her blue eyes distended, as she made some appeal. Harpey cut her short, and I saw his white teeth flash through his beard as he laughed, then he turned and departed. The girl vanished abruptly as though dragged back into the house, and the door slammed.

"Is that chauffeur a good man?" I asked Sullivan, who was still swearing to himself.

"One o' the best on the force, sir-r; it's elegant he is at the following. It's himself will shadow the old divil like a burr. Let's get over there now, right off, Mr. Clews!"

I was tempted, and hesitated. Sight of Claire Maynard had almost knocked me off my mental balance; I wanted to call a police squad and break into the house now, in broad daylight, and rescue her. Then I remembered what Lew Friedman had said—two things he had said.

"Sullivan," I returned slowly, "Harpey has set his trap and gone home. Miss Maynard won't be hurt; she'll be in danger only when you come into the trap. Lee doubtless intends to finish you both off together. To beat him, we must use our heads, not our fists."

Sullivan growled a disgusted oath. "All right, then. I been watchin' those painters workin' in back, and they're no such thing. One of 'em is Whitey Jim, a hophead and coke passer from the big town, and the other is Louie Eckers, wanted in Sacramento for forgery and in Los Angeles for crackin' an express company's safe. There's a thousand reward out for Louie. They figure they're safe enough—"

"Good!" I exclaimed. "Now I've got the key!"

"To what, sir-r?"

"Everything. Tell you later," and I laughed. Sullivan only swore again.

III

IT WAS six-thirty. A high fog had brought early darkness, and now gray obscurity was closing down on everything. In the house on the opposite corner, several lights showed. The false painters had long since knocked off work, and had departed.

Yet we had not heard from the chauffeur who had gone to shadow Harpey.

Sullivan, who had slept little the previous night, was asleep on the bed. I wakened him, and we finished off what was left of the provisions. He was sulky, and plainly resented my refusal to raid the place during the afternoon. I soon had him out of that, however.

"At seven-thirty," I told him, "you're free to act—alone or with the local police, as you think best. It'll be dangerous, because I don't know what Lee plans, but I've figured out his getaway, and what those painters were there for. Seven-thirty, remember! Until then, you sit right here. I don't like it that we've not heard from your chauffeur—"

"Where are you goin', sir-r?" demanded Sullivan as I took my hat. "And what's the getaway the divil has framed up?"

I grinned at him in the obscurity, for we had not turned on the light.

"Never mind. If I'm not back, you go ahead and act."

I left him gaping at me, and departed. From the necessities of the case, I had theorized Lee's plans, and now it remained to see whether I was right or wrong.

Once in the street, I crossed over and then started around the block, in order to reach the death-trap from the rear. Tonight, if ever, my experiences in China were to stand me in good stead, for I could speak enough of the Cantonese dialect to get by with any celestials in this country. On my way around the block, also, I found a garage—the shops were long since closed—where I bought a small saw from the wondering mechanic in charge, with some oil.

Another five minutes and I was approaching our house from the rear, along the deserted side-street. I had nearly an hour ahead of me, and was in no hurry. The airplane story, which was large enough for two rooms, was dark, and the painters' ladder stood against the rear of the roof, as though left thus until the morrow. Now or never—and I gained the ladder, mounted it swiftly, and with the oil deadening all sound, put my saw to work.

In five minutes the job was completed and I regained the ground. The house next door was a scant twenty feet away, and was dark and deserted. Crossing to it, I waited beside its rear wall. If my deductions were correct, I would not have long to wait.

I was there perhaps ten minutes, which seemed an interminable time, when two men came clumping along the side street, and I heard them admitted to the back door of Lee's house. With this, I knew that I was correct, and looked upward. It was impossible to see anything distinctly in the gloom, but presently I knew that the two men were emerging on the roof of the house and were drawing up the ladder. Then came a slight jarring noise from the roof of the house above me, and the task, by no means impossible for two men, was accomplished.

Clever enough, too! Lee, as I believed, would remain alone in the house to complete the murderous scheme; then he would escape to the roof, cross to the next house by means of the ladder, which had been laid roof to roof, and so escape. Well, forewarned was forearmed!

Then a voice startled me, and I realized that the two men had departed, but were talking in low tones.

"I'll see to it, Whitey," said one, evidently turning toward me. "You go ahead. I can slip in easy enough and make sure it's solid above. So long."

The speaker was the cracksman, Louie Eckers. An instant later I made out his figure in the gloom, so near that it startled me; he was coming to break into the empty house, gain the roof, and be certain that the ladder was well placed. The fool! To obviate this very course, Harpey had sent these men to work here during the day and become thoroughly familiar with the two houses, so that they could place that ladder without a moment's delay—and they had bungled it!

One startled oath burst from the cracksman, but only one, for my fist checked it midway. As he staggered, I drove in my left, drove it home hard and sharp, and dropped him like a log. I dropped on top of him, took two guns and an electric torch from his pockets, then got out my knife. Slitting his coat into strips, I bound him firmly hand and foot, gagged him, and rolled him to one side.

"Wassa malley?" came a thin, sharp voice, as I rose. It was that Chinese servant, who must have heard the slight scuffle, and who was approaching, "Loui! Whassa malley?"

"Be quiet and come here!" I said in Cantonese. "The master sent me to keep watch. Where is Li Toy?"

This was the Chinese name of our friend Lee, meaning Li the Talented. It was a true enough name, too. Its mention disarmed the uneasiness of the man, who approached me.

"I was leaving as ordered," he said, "when I heard the noise—"

He was no fighter, and when I took him by the throat made hardly a struggle. I choked him limp, and then tied him up and left him near Louie Eckers for future attention. His words proved that I was correct, and Lee was now alone in the house with Claire Maynard.

Then, blinded by my own exultation at having used my wits so well, I lost my head. Instead of returning for Sullivan as I had intended to do if my surmises proved correct, I turned to the house. The thought of Lee there, alone with Claire Maynard, maddened me and drove all caution from me; I had bullets for Lee, and meant to shoot him on sight, for he was like a mad dog. So why waste time and endanger the girl, when I could complete the job myself?

Thus spurred to folly, I loosened my shoes, took them off, and reached for the rear lower roof over the kitchen, which was just over my head. The windows of the upper story were certain to be unlocked, since Lee depended on them for his getaway, while nothing would be open downstairs. Without a sound I scaled the sharply inclined roof, much of which was daubed with still fresh paint, and reached the airplane story. The first window I tried was unlocked, and slid open as though oiled. The flashlight showed me an empty bedroom, and I entered, then shut the window.

A moment afterward, I was standing on a stairway which led to the lower rooms. Dim light and a sound of voices came to me, and I descended cautiously. The stairway had an abrupt elbow, and on reaching it I found that it ended in a hallway. Beside the stairs was an open doorway which emitted a flood of light. This was the dining room, and in it, although they were hidden from me, were Lee and Claire Maynard. Now I heard Lee speaking, and that soft, deadly voice of his with its ring of steel wakened a shiver of recollection in my mind.

"Go on into the library, young lady," he was saying. "Go on and make yourself comfortable, for I have work to do. No use your whining; your friend Clews is dead or in the hospital, and no one will come tonight except the detective Sullivan. Now remember! When he comes, you are to admit him—and then do what you please."

"You devil!" said the girl's voice, yet with such an accent of despair and weary futility that it made me shudder. "I believe you mean to murder him—"

"Very probably," and Lee laughed. "But if you fail to admit him, your father will be disgraced and sent to the penitentiary tomorrow! That is the bother of having a father who is a bank official and a responsible man—especially if he has failed in his duty. He thinks that you are enjoying a delightful vacation in America with your dear uncle, eh? Very nice, indeed!"

"My father has done nothing wrong," flashed the girl's voice. "If he has, then it was my uncle who tricked him into it—"

"Our friend Harpey has ways and means, assuredly," and Lee laughed again. "Well, go on into the library, if you please! When Sullivan comes, scream or do whatever you like—it is all one to me."

Peering cautiously around the corner of the stairs, I saw the girl come into the doorway of the dining-room, I had just learned a great deal about her—more of her story, indeed, than I had previously known—and I was not astounded by her attitude of utter dejection. She pulled the door of the dining-room shut behind her, crossed the hall to a second doorway, and went into the room. This, the library, was at the front of the house beside the entrance.

For an instant I hesitated, then I stole down the stairs. It was no part of my plan to walk in upon Lee, who might be in the dining-room or kitchen, anywhere in the rear of the house; I stood in a healthy respect of his abilities. My only chance to get him, was to get the drop on him first. What I did want to do, however, was to get the girl out of the house and let her know that she need not be in further fear of her uncle. Lee figured that she would scream out some warning when Sullivan did come—and that was exactly what he desired, for it would bring Sullivan inside on the jump.

So, crossing the hall noiselessly, I pushed open the library door, and came face to face with Claire Maynard, standing beneath the electric lights.

I had thought she would either scream or faint, but she did neither. She stood staring at me, a mortal pallor creeping across her face, her eyes distended. I went swiftly to her, and caught her outstretched hand. A low word broke from her.

"You! They told me you—you—"

"I'm not," I said under my breath. "This time we've got the gang where we want 'em, but you must get out of here. What's the trap, do you know? What does Lee plan to do?"

She shook her head, still staring at me.

"I don't know. It's terrible, frightful—"

"No, it isn't," I reassured her. "Have you any money?" She nodded to that. "Then get out of here at once—we don't want you tangled up in the police investigation. Get out and leave the front door open. The current of air will bring Lee, and I'll attend to him. You go to the garage around the corner and hire a car to take you to San Francisco at once. Don't delay, understand? Get off at once. Go to my friend Lew Friedman, who's been directing all this fight on Harpey. He's an old man, a cripple, a dear man! He'll protect you, see that your father is not endangered. Can you do this?"

"Yes," she breathed, with a short nod. Her face, a delicate oval contour framed in her golden hair, was very pale but composed and resolute. "Yes. Where is he, this man?"

I told her Friedman's address in Millard Street, repeated it, impressed it firmly upon her mind, while I listened for any faintest sound from the hall. None came.

"Sullivan will be here after a little—don't worry about me," I said. "I'll attend to Lee, unless Sullivan comes first. Now get out, quickly!"

"Oh, I'm so glad!" For an instant her two hands gripped mine, her eyes shone mistily into mine. "I'm so thankful—for you! I had no hope—"

"And you still have none," said Lee's soft, steely voice. Then something crashed into me, and I went down and out.

IV

I WAKENED, ONLY a moment or two later, to a frightful sight—the face of Lee just above me. It was the face of a demoniac, snarling, eyes aflame, thin and indescribably vicious. He had just finished binding and gagging me, and Claire Maynard must have flung herself frantically upon him, for he had struck her aside. She was clinging to a chair, pulling herself erect, terrified and shrinking before his eyes and voice.

"Get into the hall!" he said, motioning to the doorway. She obeyed, and he followed swiftly, dragging me by the collar. He left me lying in the doorway, half into the hall, the girl shrinking back against the opposite wall. Then, not taking his eyes from her, he retreated to the foot of the stairs. There he took a telephone receiver from the instrument hanging on the wall, and called a number.

"We'll settle you, and your friend Friedman, too!" he flung at us, and laughed. "So Sullivan will be here soon, eh? Good. It won't be any too soon for me. Ah—hello!"

Still watching the girl, he began to speak in Cantonese. And as I listened, a cold horror settled upon me, for now I knew, the worst had happened. Lew Friedman was lost.

"Yes, this is Li Toy," he said. "What? Louie has not returned? Then Captain Clews has detained him. Yes, Clews is not only alive, but is here listening. I found him in the house a moment ago. Now, listen to me! The man behind Clews is one named Friedman, a cripple of some sort—"

He broke off and grinned at us as he listened. Undoubtedly, Harpey recognized that name. He had known Friedman in China, or had known of him.

"Here is the address," went on Lee, and gave him the address which I had imparted to Claire Maynard. "You had better clear out—there's no telling how much Clews has learned. What's that? Followed you from here today? Oh, all right; I hope you did the job well. Eh? Good. Yes, Sullivan is coming here soon now, and then I'll be on my way. Don't wait for me. Clear out at once; drop everything and run for it. Good-by. *Ho hang la!*"

He chuckled and hung up the receiver. Even then, I believe that he was enjoying his little joke, frightening Harpey into making a dash for it. As for me, I now knew why the police chauffeur had never reported back to us. Harpey had caught him in some trap and had killed him mercilessly. That was Harpey's way.

My head was still ringing, aching cruelly, blood running over my skull as I lay. Lee must have given me a fearful crack with a slungshot. I could not regard this, however; not even that horrible blood-lusting visage of Lee had any further chill for me, after what had just been said. *Harpey knew!* And as sure as

I lay there, I felt that the death-warrant of Lew Friedman had been sealed.

Now Lee stepped backward to the stairs and stood there, grinning. From his pocket he took an object and began to play with it. I could not make out what it was. Perfectly certain of his own escape, confident in his own ability, the yellow devil was in an exultant mood. His soft laugh had the deadly ring of tempered steel.

"These are useful little things," he observed. "Useful little things, Captain Clews! I believe you introduced them into the Chinese army, some time ago? Yes, when Sullivan bursts in, this will be very useful When the pin is pulled out—you comprehend?"

"A grenade!" The low cry broke from Claire Maynard, as she pressed back against the wall, white as death; and her words apprised me as to the nature of the object. Lee again laughed softly.

At this instant, as I lay there on the floor with freezing horror clutching at me, I heard a slight sound from outside. Sullivan was there! Frantically, I writhed in my bonds, to no avail. Oh, to warn Sullivan out of this! The instant he opened the door, we were all lost! Lee would drop the grenade, leap up the stairs—

"Yes, and look at it well!" Lee held up the grenade, jeeringly. The terrorized girl drew back against the wall, hands outspread gropingly. "Look at it well, young lady! When you next see it, it will be for one little instant, but the pin will be out—and then you will see nothing else! Look at it well—"

A hand from outside tried the doorknob, turned it. Lee's gaze flashed to the door, as he caught the sound.

At this instant Claire Maynard moved. Her arm whirled like a white flash above me. Swift as light, her groping hand had caught a framed picture from the wall, had hurled it. It curved through the air, even as Lee's other hand came up to the grenade—and struck against his two hands. The bomb fell intact, rolled down across the floor of the hall. A scream broke from the girl.

The front door was burst open and the figure of Sullivan towered there. Lee had no chance to recover his grenade and pull the pin—with one hoarse shriek of fury, he leaped up the stairs. Sullivan saw him, fired, missed. Lee was around the elbow of the stairway and gone, like a foiled ghost, leaving a trail of snarled oaths behind him.

For a moment I could comprehend things very dimly—I was near to fainting, for once in my life. Claire Maynard lay in a limp heap. I heard Sullivan shouting above me, heard other men tramping and calling out as they pounded up the stairs. Sullivan was leaning over me, cutting me free, one of the local policemen helping him.

"We've got him—he's upstairs now, sir-r!" he cried out, as he aided me to stagger up. "Glory be, are ye bad hurt?"

I leaned back against the wall and began to laugh, hysterically. It frightened poor Sullivan, who caught me and shook me. That brought the pain to my head, and I groaned.

"You've not got him," I gasped out. "Outside, quick—between the houses—come on!"

I staggered to the doorway, Sullivan catching my arm, and from my pocket drew out the electric torch I had taken form the cracksman. Like a drunken man, I reeled down the steps and got to the corner of the house. Then, from somewhere up above, came a rending crack of wood, a single wild, shrill cry echoing upon the darkness, and then a terrible dead sound. I pressed on the torch, and its ray caught the dark shape of Lee lying motionless on the ground, by the fragments of the ladder. He was alive, but knocked senseless, his leg broken.

"Glory be," cried Sullivan, after getting the bracelets on him. "What's it mean!"

"It means that I used a saw on his ladder," I said—and then, indeed, I fainted dead away.

V

MY EYES opened on daylight. I stared around, found white walls all about me, found the genial, heavy face of Sullivan looking down on me, realized that I lay in a hospital bed. A nurse moved, spoke quietly to Sullivan.

"All right, he's awake. Tell him everything, and get it done with."

Sullivan came to the side of the bed and gripped my fingers. Then I remembered.

"Friedman, Friedman!" I said frantically. "Get word to him at once—Harpey knows everything and—"

"It's all right, sir-r," said Sullivan, with a wide grin. "Miss Maynard heard enough to be guessin' the rest, and I looked after things right off. Telephoned the city, had a squad sent to Mr. Friedman's house, had every road watched for Harpey. Just had a message from Mr. Friedman for you, sir-r, to say himself is all right."

I relaxed weakly. "And—Miss Maynard?"

"She's waitin' outside, sir-r," said Sullivan, with another grin. "Wid a bit o' luck, the doctor says ye can travel tomorrow, and we'll all go to the city together, the three of us. Glory be, sir, the newspaper byes is fair runnin' us all wild! It's a captain of detectives I'll be, and it's a hero yourself is, and praise be to the saints all is well and sound! Lee's alive and in jail until he's taken back to the pen at San Quentin, and there's two thousand comin' to us from that, and another grand for Louie Eckers, and the little Chink ye left tied up was wanted for two tong murders in Chinatown, and the Hip Sueys have three thousand on him, I hear—"

"Never mind all that," I said, dizzy with so much news. "Where's Miss Maynard? That's what matters to me—"

And then I saw the girl's face smiling at me, and the touch of her hand gave me peace.

VI

THE HEAD OF A GHOST

*No One But a Master Genius of the Crook
World Could Have Planned the Revenge
That Harpey Was to Take on His Worst
Enemy, No One Could Guess the Result*

I

HARPEY knew the truth!
As I sat at the breakfast table with Lew Friedman, going over the morning papers, the same thought was in our two minds. Harpey knew that this man who sat across the table from me, this man with the crippled spine, this man with the mane of white hair and the keen blue eyes, was the man whose brain had caused his downfall. The newspapers did not know this fact, though every paper in San Francisco was full of the general news—but Harpey knew it.

"We'll hear from Harpey," said Friedman quietly, his eyes striking at me.

"Impossible," I said. "He's being hunted like an animal all over this section of California. He can't escape, for he's a big giant of a man with a tangle of gray beard and can't hide himself. We've got complete confessions out of those of his gang who weren't killed; his lieutenant is going to the gallows; we've located his headquarters in San José and cleaned out all his papers, money and everything else. We've unearthed details on all the jobs he has pulled off. He's down and out, and will give all his attention to getting away rather than to avenge himself on you. That sort of thing isn't done in real life. And besides, Lew, we've got two headquarters men watching this house day and night."

Friedman only nodded, a smile playing about his thin lips. He relaxed in his wheelchair and patted down the pillows.

"No use, Dick Clews! I know better," he said. "I knew Harpey in China, and with his back to the wall he's a wild beast. Knowing, as he does, that I've been responsible for tracking him down, he'll be wild to get back at me. Don't imagine, either, that he's down and out. Far from it! He's a man of tremendous mental ability, and he's no one-track crook; he's been engaged in everything from opium smuggling to political assassination. Well, let it go now. Here's the mail, and here's Miss Maynard."

The nurse came into the dining-room, bringing some letters and cables, and with her came Claire Maynard, whose father held a responsible banking post in China. It was she who really brought about Harpey's fall, since she had gained us copies of the orders he sent his lieutenant. She was supposed to be traveling in the United States with Harpey, her uncle, but in reality he had coerced her into helping him, using her as a blind and then trying to murder her. Fortunately, we had her safely away from him.

"Good morning, everybody!" she exclaimed brightly. "You're looking fine and rested this morning, Mr. Friedman! Any news yet?"

"Presently, young lady," said Friedman, with a glance at the nurse and servant. "News can wait, but eggs can't. We'll have a cablegram from China in this batch of mail, I hope."

There was good reason for his waiting until we were alone. Among Harpey's papers we had found the reason for his hold over Claire. A year previously, Harpey cleverly tricked her father into signing a document which supposedly proved him a forger—then had threatened the girl that he would expose her father unless she aided his schemes. Alone in America with the man she thought to be her uncle, fearing disgrace and exposure for her father, she acquiesced, trying to buy that document with her services. Until meeting me and Lew Friedman, she had been hopeless.

We ate in silence, Friedman tearing open the cables and letters and glancing at them. Once, I saw his expression change slightly; his thin lips drew together, a sudden glint came into his eyes, and a slight flush rose in his cheeks, but he laid down the letter that had caused this emotion without a comment. He did not speak until the nurse followed his servant from the room, then he looked up at the girl and smiled.

"A cable from your father, Miss Maynard," he said quietly. "Harpey is not your mother's brother, as you supposed, but her half-brother. Unfortunately, your father appears to have had misplaced confidence in him. There is now nothing more to fear, I assure you."

He extended the cable message to her. When she had read it, the girl rose and came over to Lew's wheelchair. She took his hand in hers, tears standing on her cheeks, and then turned and extended her other hand to me.

"I owe you two men everything," she said quietly. "I—I can't thank you enough for what you've done. Now it seems like an evil dream, my being with that man—"

"It's all forgotten, my dear," said Friedman, smiling and patting her hand. "It's all over, and we'll take care of you. But don't waste any gratitude on that big rascal across the table. He's a soldier of fortune, an adventurer, and—"

Smiling, the girl stooped and checked his words with a kiss on the lips, then she flung me one radiant look and was gone from the room. Lew Friedman leaned back in his chair, vastly surprised, and laughed a little.

"Heigh-ho!" he said, then sighed. "Daydreams, Dick, daydreams! Now she's off to have a cry in peace. Good thing, too. Shove me into the library, will you? I want a book."

He reached out to the pile of mail, and took the letter which had caused his change of expression. I pushed his chair through into the library, aware of a subtle tenseness in the air of my old friend, and there got the table adjusted across his chair. He directed me to a book on the wall shelves, stacked high with Chinese tomes, and when I got it down it was with a curious sense of fatality. It was the Chinese Gloss in which he had been wont to trace the characters used in the cipher between Harpey and the latter's lieutenant.

Friedman looked up at me, unsmiling.

"I said this morning that we'd hear from Harpey," he observed quietly. I knew that he was unafraid—not half so afraid as I was, because I realized how very little it would take to snuff out his frail life.

"I said we'd hear from him, Clews, and we've heard. Here's the letter—look it over while I go after the meaning. It was like him to send me a message in the same code he used for Lee— like him!"

From the paper he handed me, a single Chinese character stared up, brushed in red ink.

That was all the message. No signature was needed. Harpey was an exquisite calligraphist, and Friedman had known instantly whose hand brushed this crimson message.

As to what the character meant, that was another thing. It was no common one, or Friedman would have recognized it instantly. No matter what the concrete meaning might be, it had for me at least a more terrible abstract meaning; it signified that Harpey was safe and among friends, ready to turn his attention to vengeance, ready to strike at the man who had hunted him down and destroyed his criminal activities.

Lew Friedman closed the book and shoved it aside; he was pale and drawn. Relaxing in his chair, he looked up at me with a weary smile, and silently gestured toward his brass writing case. I laid it before him. He took up a brush, wet it, filled it with the Chinese ink, and deftly laid down lines on a sheet of paper. There before me grew the ancient and primitive Chinese pictography of which the modern character was an abbreviation due to the countless scribes who had copied it across the centuries. Friedman pointed with his brush to the three objects which composed the picture.

"Very simple after all, Dick, and only what was to be expected. Here at the top is the head of a ghost; below that to the left, a claw-foot; and to the right a man in the attitude of fright. For, as the Gloss explains it, nothing inspires such terror in a man as the head of a ghost and the claw of a tiger. True enough. And there's the little message that Harpey has sent us, the one word *wei*. One word can mean a lot sometimes, Dick."

"Bosh!" I said abruptly. "He can't reach you in any possible way, Lew, and you know it. He's helpless to touch you."

Friedman shrugged a little. "I hope so, because I can't resist him. I might fire a pistol at him, but the shock of the recoil would pretty near finish me, I'm afraid. I—"

"Forget this!" I commanded angrily. "He's trying to work on you, that's what it is—trying to reach your mind, since he can't reach your body!"

Friedman nodded, and his eyes flashed. "Perhaps you're right, Dick. Very well, I'll do as you say—forget it!"

II

IT WAS all very well for me to order Lew Friedman to forget that message, but I could not forget it. In my mind lingered a vaguely uneasy conviction that this one-word message held more than a mere warning; that it held some ghastly hint which we were destined to remember later on—when Harpey struck. And Lew Friedman entertained the same idea, though he made no further reference to the message, and we told Claire Maynard nothing of it.

However, I took precautions. Friedman could not be moved from the house; his condition was so far on the mend that his doctor had called in a surgeon and they were considering an operation which might cure him, in case he gathered strength enough to stand it, and to this end he must remain quiet. He was safe enough here, in any event—as safe as anywhere. I visited police headquarters, explained the situation, and was assured that the guard of two detectives would remain on duty indefinitely. It was little enough to do for a man, as the chief said, who had rid the city and state of such a criminal gang.

I did not lack for money, since from the rewards and incidental gleanings a large amount had been reaped. So we placed Claire Maynard with a family next door, under various pretenses, until we should get instructions from her father; she was determined to remain here until the issue of Friedman's operation became known. This left me in the house with Lew and a trained nurse, and a servant who went home at night. With the two detectives always on the watch, we seemed in perfect security—but both Lew Friedman and I settled down to wait. We said nothing of it, kept our apprehensions to ourselves, yet we both knew Harpey.

Thus passed three days, uneventfully.

On the fourth morning the surgeon called and minutely examined Friedman. He gave his verdict for an immediate operation, to which Lew assented gladly. The surgeon was one of the best in the city, a man of international reputation, and gave us every hope that the operation would put my old friend on his feet again in a month's time.

"Very well," he said, when Lew told him to go ahead. "I'll operate at three this afternoon, at the Mt. Zion hospital. I'll send the ambulance at two-thirty, we'll put you right on the table, and you'll be done in a jiffy!"

Claire Maynard at once insisted on going along, but this was promptly vetoed. At last, to keep her engaged, it was settled that she should go on to the hospital and get Friedman's room ready and decorated with flowers and anything else that suited her, so the surgeon took her away with him in his car. I was going in the ambulance with Lew, of course.

All this relieved me mightily. Not alone because of the good prospect for Friedman, but because in the hospital he would be absolutely safe from Harpey, and would be there for three weeks or so. By that time, I hoped to have Harpey where he belonged. I had already arranged to comb Chinatown with a squad from headquarters, as we figured this to be his most likely hiding place, due to his long acquaintance with China and with the worst type of Chinese criminals in this country, who were all hand in glove with him.

Miss Maynard called up about noon that everything was ready at the hospital and that she was lunching there. After lunch the nurse and I got Lew ready for the move, and two o'clock had just sounded when an ambulance climbed the steep Millard Street hill and stopped before the house.

"You're ahead of time," I said to the two attendants who brought in the stretcher.

"Yes, sir," replied one. "There's a big emergency case at the hospital—automobile crash on Post Street—and Doctor Smith wants to bring Mr. Friedman to his own house. He has an operating room there and is getting everything in shape."

"That's good of him, certainly," I said, and we fell to work.

In five minutes we had Lew on the stretcher, got him into the ambulance, and slung the stretcher in cushioned slings. The chauffeur, I observed, was an intelligent young Chinese, which is nothing unusual in San Francisco, and he tooled the car like a veteran. Friedman never felt the least shock, as we got down the hill and started west.

We were not far from the Presidio when we reached our destination—a house behind low walls, oddly enough, on a steep hill street. Our friend the surgeon lived in an expensive neighborhood, I reflected; then, as there was no porte-cochère, we lifted out the stretcher and carried Friedman up from the gate to the front door of the house. The door was opened to us, by a Chinese servant, who touched my arm.

"Mr. Clews? The docto' say you wait in here a minute," and he indicated a door down the hall to the left.

It was natural enough that the surgeon would not want me messing around in his operating room before the ceremony began, so I said a temporary good-by to Lew and went into the side room. The servant closed the door after me, and I looked around.

The room was very small, lighted only by a small high window, and was a library, the walls shelved with books to the ceiling on all sides. Medical works, I presumed, but saw my error as I looked more closely at the titles of the volumes; this little room contained a marvelous collection of works on crim-inology, in half a dozen languages, many of them abstruse scientific tomes. Rather an odd hobby for a great surgeon, I thought, and noted that the volumes appeared well thumbed and used. Idly, I took down one of them and looked for his name—but there was none. Instead of a name on the fly-leaf, I saw several Chinese characters brushed there.

Something in the look of those characters, in the delicate precision, the consummate artistry, with which they were brushed, startled me. I replaced the book and went to the door, realizing that time had passed since I had entered.

The door was locked.

It was a massive, solid door and did not yield an iota to my shaking. I paused, staring at it, incredulous yet wildly alarmed. In a flash, the whole sequence of events shot through my mind—the arrival of the ambulance before the set time, the Chinese chauffeur, our coming to this private house, my sepa-ration from Friedman, and finally the name brushed in Chinese writing in those books dealing with crime. Then, too late, it came to me what that name must be, why I was locked in this cell of a room.

A slight sound drew my attention, and I turned. Behind me, three tiers of volumes had vanished; in place of them I saw an opening, in which was framed the naked torso of a yellow man. Something fell about my neck, drew taut. I gripped at it with unavailing fingers, tried to shout, felt myself dragged sideways. With a thrill of horror, I recognized that the fine silk line which had noosed me was the cord of the executioner.

Harpey had struck!

III

UPON THAT one instant of time hung everything. More from despair and bitter shock than from any intent, I went limp and let myself be dragged toward the wall. The slender cord was biting into my neck; a feeling of lassitude, of horrible futility, left me helpless. The realization of Harpey's superhuman cunning overpowered me for the moment and numbed me in every nerve and muscle. I could not think or act. There was a gun in my coat pocket, yet I was absolutely incapable of even trying to get it. Withal, my brain was quite clear. As I went down, I had a glimpse of a bare little room adjoining the library, with two Chinese stripped to the waist, and recognized one as the house-servant who had admitted me, the other as the chauffeur of the ambulance.

Then I was against the wall, and both of them were coming through the opening to fall upon me. The servant held the cord and stood up to draw it tighter, while the chauffeur rolled me over and knelt on my back. That they meant to finish me then and there was quite apparent. Already my lungs were bursting, sparks began to dance before my eyes, and the frightful torture of suffocation was upon me.

Now, paradoxical as it might seem, my own helplessness came to the rescue. Taking for granted that I was down and out, the servant gave the cord an instant's slack to get a better grip, and flung a jest at his companion. That brief instant of time gave me a gulp of air, and brought me back to sanity.

My reaction was frantic, almost spasmodic. With my out-stretched hand I clutched the ankle of the servant, and at the same time gave my body a sharp twist and heave. So unex-pected was the movement that it caught the two murderers off guard. The servant fell headlong, and the man kneeling on me was pitched sideways; as he went over, my foot caught him full in the side and doubled him up in agony.

I rolled over, and came to my knees. From the servant broke a sharp yelp, and then another—he was yelling for help. He had kept hold of the cord, and now drew in upon it with the intent of finishing his task, as he scrambled across the little room to drag it taut. I plunged forward, got to my feet, and he was an instant too late to pull me down. Next moment my fist caught him under the chin and drove him headlong into the massive door. He fell and lay quiet, his head twisted askew—his neck was broken.

So far, so good—I was caught like a rat in a trap, and done for, but now I meant to fight before they got me down. Others would be here soon enough. As I turned, the chauffeur was dragging himself to one knee. A brave devil like most of his race, he was gasping for breath and drawing out a pistol as he gasped. I kicked the pistol away, then gave him my toe under the ear and he flopped over like a dying fish. He was out for keeps this time.

Panting, I leaned against the book-shelves and dragged the cord from about my neck. Then I got out my pistol, and waited. Nothing happened. The complete silence gradually impressed me; perhaps, after all, the noise and yelps had not been heard! If so, I had a chance.

My brain woke up, grasped certain aspects of the affair. Ob-viously, Harpey had none too many men with him, since they were doubling their rôles, and it was probable that he trusted none except Chinese. Those two stretcher-bearers were not frauds—they had been rented with the ambulance for the occasion. Therefore, since no alarm had been caused by the confusion here, Harpey must have only a few men on hand, and these must be busy elsewhere. At this thought I went cold, with memory of Friedman. No wonder Harpey was too busy to waste any time on me!

At any rate, I was free, armed, and now knew exactly what to expect. Since there was no sign of alarm, I could count on making my escape—but now I had no such thought. If Lew Friedman was dead, then I would certainly get the murderer; if not, I had a chance to save him, or at least to make the essay.

Glancing into the bare little cupboard of a room adjoining this library cell, I saw that it had a small door and was lighted by electricity. Then I went to the body of the house-servant and in his trousers found several keys. Of these, one opened the door of my prison. I stepped out into the hall, closed the door behind me, and got my bearings.

Friedman had been carried on to the end of this hall, which was a long one, past the staircase that ascended; therefore, he had not been taken upstairs. A dead silence appeared to reign in the house, which was an old one, built in the lofty style that had obtained before the fire. The hall was obscure, as the light came through stained glass panels.

I started toward the rear; then, in a curtained recess, my eye caught the outline of a wall telephone. Instantly I decided to take the chance, and stepped to it. It was with a gulp of untold relief, as though coming again into a world of sanity, that I heard the clear "Number, please?" of the operator.

The chief of police in a great city, like the President of the United States, can be reached swiftly and directly on the wire, if one knows the right number. Fortunately, I did, and in thirty seconds I heard the chief's voice. I told him softly who I was.

"My lord, man!" he exploded. "We've been hunting for you and Friedman—never showed up at the hospital."

"Harpey has us," I said. "We're near the Presidio. I don't know whether Friedman is alive or not. I don't know the street, but—"

I described the house and its location as well as possible. He began to press me for further details, but just then I heard a soft sound from the hallway, outside my curtained recess, and a voice spoke in Chinese.

"Is that you, Wu Lung? Is the white devil dead?"

"He is with his ancestors," I returned, in the singsong Cantonese, hung up the receiver, and went to the curtains. Within arm's reach of me was a coolie, thin and scrawny and marked by opium.

"Oh son of turtles," he responded, "make haste to the master at once!"

"With pleasure," I said, and had him by his long neck.

He squirmed like an eel, whipped out a long knife, and gave me a nasty cut across the back before he collapsed. I carried him to the library door, threw him inside with the other two, and locked the door. Then I started down the hall again, toward a curtain at the farther end, through which I thought the man had come.

Behind the curtain was a door standing slightly ajar, proving my surmise accurate. I found myself in a small, dark passage with another door at the far end, and went on to it. Gun in hand, I quietly turned the knob and found another heavy curtain fronting me. I pushed this aside, closing the door behind me— and found myself in a pitch-dark chamber.

A cry of horror came to my lips at the thing I saw there in the darkness, but I checked it and stood motionless, trying to get a grip on myself. Now I realized the double meaning in that grim message from Harpey. There before me, seeming to float in mid-air, luminous with an incandescent and ghostly light, was a disembodied head; it was a horrible gaunt visage that I saw, bitterly cruel, clean-shaven and betraying with merciless clarity every line of the high-boned features—the head of Harpey!

IV

HOW LONG I stood there gaping at this ghastly apparition is hard to say. I was unseen, unheard, for the door had closed silently and I made no sound as I gripped the curtain and stared. Then a voice came out of the darkness to complete my paralysis, for it was Friedman's voice, cool and deliberate as ever. It seemed to come from close by in the obscurity.

"You're surprisingly childish, Harpey. You ought to know that all this mummery does not worry me in the least. If you're going to stick that knife into me, then go ahead and do it, and stop talking."

Evidently I had come in at the end of a conversation. Harpey laughed and replied. His tones were deep, rich, fully expressive of his powerful personality, and fairly filled the chamber with sonorous vibration.

"Not in the darkness. Besides, this is not entirely for your benefit, my dear Friedman, but also for that of my assistants."

There was something indescribably horrible in the gibbering movements of that floating face with its black eyesockets, in hearing the words that issued from those incandescent lips— but by this time I was back to earth again. Harpey had merely staged a reception with the aid of a darkened room and some radium paint, perhaps hoping to shake Friedman's nerve as well as to impress his own Chinese servants.

But Lew Friedman was still alive—that was the great thing! He was somewhere near by me, no doubt waiting for death. He spoke again, and his voice thrilled me anew.

"Since you've got me, Harpey, at least let Clews go. Don't murder him—"

"Your appeal is too late," returned Harpey. "Clews is dead. Now, having finished our conversation, I suppose that we may come to business. The lights, Li Szu!"

At these words, I swiftly shoved open the door behind me and drew myself behind the curtain, my gun ready. It was in my mind to shoot Harpey down without hesitation, but I could not afford to make mistakes; and how many men he had on hand, I did not know. There was the click of an electric switch, and upon the blackness burst a dazzling flood of radiance. I was well concealed behind the heavy curtain, but when I peered around its fringed border, I received a fresh shock.

Whatever this chamber had originally been, Harpey had exercised his diabolic cunning and had converted it into a mock operating room, snowy white everywhere; he had the knack of doing amazing things on short notice. I could just see the end of the operating table on which lay Friedman, and beside it the figure of Harpey. A ghastly figure it was, too, clad in a long white apron; the face was a greenish yellow in hue from the luminous paint, and in the outstretched hand was a murderous scalpel. Shorn of its flowing gray beard, Harpey's visage was a gauntly hideous thing, stamped with evil cruelty. I saw him wave the scalpel and grin at Friedman.

"Presently we shall turn you over and I shall perform this charmingly delicate operation, my dear Friedman! I know you will be delighted to have me do so. First, however, there is a detail not yet completed; I have something I must show you. Li Szu, go and tell Wu Lung to hurry here with the head of that foreign devil."

These last words were uttered in rapid Cantonese. Before I could comprehend their meaning, before I could move, the curtain was suddenly dashed aside from my left, and a yellow man caromed into me. Instead of recoiling, he instantly grappled with me, flung his weight against me, and we went down together. Caught between our bodies, the curtain came along over us and enveloped the two of us in its folds, wrapping me about the head and arms. Not, however, before I had glimpsed that Harpey had no other assistants in the room.

In that blinking embrace, with the yellow devil clawing frantically at me, I was as good as lost. I shoved the pistol against the heaving body and fired, felt Li Szu relax and heard him cough as he died—yet I could not get free of that curtain. Then something struck me like a whirlwind, and I knew that Harpey was on me.

By good fortune, as it proved, the body of Li Szu was still enlaced with mine. Harpey was launching terrific kicks at the two of us, trying to knock my pistol away beneath the curtain— and he did it. His toe reached my elbow with numbing force. Next instant he picked both of us up bodily and, with a bestial howl of sheer fury, actually hurled us across the room. He had the strength of a gorilla in those great arms of his.

The dead yellow man saved me from the greatest force of the fall; nonetheless, as we crashed down, I was left dazed for the moment. The curtain fell away from my head, a roar like the scream of a maddened animal filled the room, and I saw Harpey leaping for me. All his calm had departed. Now he was slavering incoherent howls of fury, his eyes were blazing in that awful greenish face, and the ferocity of his attack was appalling. I had time for nothing but to writhe out of his way and kick his feet from under him as he landed.

He crashed into the wall, and I had a chance to gain my feet. My pistol was somewhere on the floor, and as good as a mile away, for Harpey spun about and hurled himself at me with the scalpel reaching out. I met him with a knockout smash on the point of his jaw, and it did not even stagger him. He caught hold of me with one hand while the other drove the scalpel for my throat.

The razor-steel bit deep, and I heard a low cry from Friedman as the blood sprang—but a twist saved the jugular and I gripped Harpey's wrist. I might as well have tried to grip a cyclone. He tore free and plunged the blade at me again, his slavering mask of fury within a foot of my face, sheer madness flaming in his eyes. This time I caught the steel in my left arm as I fended my throat, and Harpey snarled as he jerked it loose and thrust anew.

I had been hitting him, but absolutely without result. Every man has his weak point, however, and as Harpey thrust in to finish me, I drove home a weighty kick to his shin and broke away from him. Ducking under his arm, I landed a smash at the angle of his big jaw which knocked him into the wall, then turned and made a plunge for where I thought the pistol would be. By this time I knew it was a finish fight.

To my dismay, there was no pistol in sight. I met Lew Friedman's horrified eyes for a brief instant, as he held himself up on the operating table and stared—then Harpey was after me, howling and roaring oaths.

"Under the chair, Dick!" pierced Friedman's voice, but I had no time to obey.

Harpey came on with a leap. I gave him all I had, in a terrific smash that landed flush on his jaw, and it never even worried him. He wound his left hand in my coat lapel, and landed one swipe with the steel that left a red gash right across my breast. I tried to kick again, and failed. Then, as the scalpel flamed for my throat, I got a foot against the wall behind me, lowered my head, and shoved forward.

Not even Harpey could resist that, and we went in a wild plunge across the floor, both of us twisting and clawing madly as we rolled. I felt my strength going, and exerted the last ounce of it to finish him, but to no avail. Another roll, and he landed on top of me, flashed up the scalpel, and drove it down furiously.

I jerked my head. The blade missed, made a slight gash in my neck, and shattered as it slammed into the hardwood floor. Harpey snarled, wrapped his big hands around my throat, and began to squeeze; a demoniac grin came on his face as I struck vainly at him, and he realized that he had me. I realized it, too, for I was unable to move under his weight, and for the second time in an hour things began to go black around me.

"Under the chair, Dick, the chair!" came Friedman's voice.

No use—Harpey had me. My neck seemed breaking under the grip of those throttling fingers, and even the devilish face above me was receding into nowhere. I beat the floor frantically with feet and hands. My right wrist struck something—the rung of a chair just above it. With a last glimmering of sense, I groped blindly and desperately around, and felt my fingers close on the lost pistol.

Of what happened after that, I have no memory.

V

I OPENED MY eyes, sniffed arnica and other things, and realized that I was in a hospital bed. Also, I had been there for some time, because it was growing dark. I was wrapped in bandages like King Tut and could not move—but I was obviously alive.

The door opened, and in came the surgeon, Doctor Smith.

"Hello, waked up, have you?" he exclaimed. "Upon my word, you're a tough devil! I had to use a sewing-machine to stitch you up, while those two bullets you put into Harpey—"

"Where's Friedman?" I croaked. Talking was painful.

"Next room," he said, and chuckled. "The operation was a complete success."

"I've heard that before," I said huskily. "You've operated? Will he live?"

"You bet your life he will," said the surgeon cheerfully. "But your friend Harpey won't. He's about passing out now. Too bad we couldn't save him for the chair. Well, here's someone who wants to see you. I'll give you just five minutes, and no more today."

He turned and beckoned. Into the room came Claire Maynard, and stooped beside me, and—well, we made good use of that five minutes. If you don't believe it, ask Mrs. Dick Clews!

ABOUT THE AUTHOR

H. BEDFORD-JONES is a Canadian by birth, but not by profession, having removed to the United States at the age of one year. For over twenty years he has been more or less profitably engaged in writing and traveling. As he has seldom resided in one place longer than a year or so and is a person of retiring habits, he is somewhat a man of mystery; more than once he has suffered from unscrupulous gentlemen who impersonated him—one of whom murdered a wife and was subsequently shot by the police, luckily after losing his alias.

The real Bedford-Jones is an elderly man, whose gray hair and precise attire give him rather the appearance of a retired foreign diplomat. His hobby is stamp collecting, and his collection of Japan is said to be one of the finest in existence. At present writing he is en route to Morocco, and when this appears in print he will probably be somewhere on the Mojave Desert in company with Erle Stanley Gardner.

Questioned as to the main facts in his life, he declared there was only one main fact, but it was not for publication; that his life had been uneventful except for numerous financial losses, and that his only adventures lay in evading adventurers. In his younger years he was something of an athlete, but the encroachments of age preclude any active pursuits except that of motoring. He is usually to be found poring over his stamps, working at his typewriter, or laboring in his California rose garden, which is one of the sights of Cathedral Cañon, near Palm Springs.